THE LAND BETWEEN TIMES

THE FIRST OF THE LAND, AND THE FIRST COMBINED ARMY

Kasper Endelt

First published in Great Britain by
L.R. Price Publications Ltd., 2020.

This edition published by
L.R. Price Publications Ltd.,
27 Old Gloucester Street,
London, WC1N 3AX
www.lrpricepublications.com

ISBN13: 978-183806101-2

THE LAND BETWEEN TIMES

THE FIRST OF THE LAND, AND THE FIRST COMBINED ARMY

Kasper Endelt

Introduction

An old, hooded man sits in a chair behind a desk. Before him is a book empty of words, along with a pen and ink. He stares at the book, with a weary sigh. Then, laboriously, he picks up his pen. Eventually, he starts to write.

He narrates aloud as he writes, much as one would if reading his story for another. The old, hooded man speaks slowly...

"My name is Magg Mage Maggtu. I created and I rule the Land of Time – a land between time itself. Along with my time mages, who then numbered ten, I manage the land and ensure the prosperous lives of the people and creatures who live upon it. In these pages, I will tell you how all of those people came to be, or were later born, in the Land of Time.

"But, first, permit me to describe the land itself:

"Sedrak is a land of water and seas. Sandler is a land of sand and heat. Grarss is fertile land, of forest and grassy meadows. Rroker is the land of mountains and rock. Svaplar is the land of swamps, full of fog and stench. The Golden Forest bears leaves as shiny as gold, and trees as solid as a diamond, but one side of the forest has turned dark – an occurrence which will be indulged later in this account. Barlar is a barren land, covered by volcanoes, where nothing grows but the cracks in the ground. Icres is a land of ice and snow, and is the home of the time mages' tower.

"To enlighten the reader as to the situation of each land in respect of the other, consider that Rroker lies dead centre, in the Land of Time... To the north is the land of Grarss, and north of that is Icres. To the south of Rroker lies the Golden Forest, and to the south of the forest lies Sandler. Further south still of that lies Sedrak. To the east of Rroker is Svaplar, and to the west lies Barlar.

"Each land is as large as a continent, as you may know it on your own Earth. Each is shaped in its own image. I originally planned to make it into my own, but abandoned this pursuit, instead allowing the land to evolve naturally, and let its species develop as they please. Still, though, I sent my time mages down, to ensure its randomness was just so sufficiently controlled, and to serve as my own eyes and ears.

"Then, let the tale unfold. I shall tell you of the first of the land; those who came in the beginning, to shape it into what it now is, alongside their enemies. I will also tell you of how they came to combine their armies.

"I know all and I am all. I am the Lord of Time; let my tale unfold before you."

And, with those words, the old man waves his hands over the book, as it begins to glow; a mixture of blue and white light, which swirls together and forms shape, before becoming a living picture...

Chapter One

The Elves

We will start at the beginning, with the first to arrive: the Elves.

It all began in the Golden Forest, where the trees and their leaves shine gold. Twenty Elves arrived in the Golden Forest, through a time portal which I crafted from the destroyed land of Emirie. Their king was Tiri Darari Kinnar, a tall, slim Elven man, some three-and-a-half metres tall. He was followed by ten women and ten men. They set about making the forest their home, with Elven magic, and when this was done, they used their magic to make their huts from the trees, which yet remained living and healthy.

I sent my first mage, Larue, down to talk to them, as my representative, my voice and my will. But, before I give account of this encounter, I will afford you a look into the world of the Elves, and what was happening to them at the very moment before a portal opened, and I was successful at getting them inside.

I found them in the realm of Erismaly, which translates roughly to "where lovely trees grow". An army of big, red, three-metre-high brutes were driving back these tall, slim, sharp-eared people, toward some sort of ruins. Although the Elves fired off barrage after barrage of arrows, they gained no ground, nor held their own; farther and farther toward the wall behind them they were pushed, as they fought gallantly but in vain to make ground.

The Elven magic was barely helping. Roots and saplings shot from the ground to impale some of the red brutes, but more just kept coming. As if to metaphorize the hopeless struggle, a black cloud was forming outside of the ruins, epitomizing the growing fear of the Elves.

Yet, just as all looked lost, a mass of glowing white and blue appeared, swirling to form a circle, and a voice started to call out from it – a voice of hope, inviting them to safety. Seeing their only hope for escape, the Elves did not hesitate, and immediately began their retreat into the portal. Only twenty made it through, before the ruins were inevitably overrun.

In the Golden Forest, a portal opened up, and the Elves made their exit into a wood of golden colour.

There they found a lone, young, Human-looking man, sitting there as one of their own. Tiri, wearing a crown of leaves and twigs, was the first aware of the mage's presence, and proceeded over to talk with him.

"Ir torein Mentya mogein felan."

Larue replied: "I am the voice of Magg Mage Maggtu. Pray to Him and He will guide you. Let me give you the gift of time langue; o, Great Lord of Time, teach these people your langue."

And, at that, I gave them the gift of time langue.

Tiri addressed me through Larue: "I thank you for this gift to my people. As He is the one who sent us here, we will obey Him, but we will not abandon our own beliefs." With this pledge, Tiri bowed elegantly.

"Good," Larue replied, "He expects nothing less. I will now be on my way, but when new people come, be sure to help them along the right path."

Tiri nodded his head in assent. "As the Time Lord commands."

Larue tapped his stick on the ground twice, before disappearing into thin air.

*

As time passed, that population of twenty grew to two-hundred-plus adult Elves and over 150 children. For a while, they led a simple and prosperous existence.

But, before long, a corrupt time mage had reopened the portal, and something evil was able to slip through. I sent a messenger to Larue, to return to help the Elves.

At the Time Tower, Larue was deep in prayer when he heard his master's message: "My first mage, you must go and warn the Elves that an old enemy is near. They must destroy the evil which pursues them from their home-world."

Larue bowed his head and answered the command: "As you command, Time Master; your will shall be done."

Larue arrived out of nowhere, in the middle of the Elven city we now know as Earasira. He immediately set to summoning the elusive people.

"Elves, come to me; I command you in the name of Magg Mage Maggtu!"

The Elves began to appear, in the trees and in the ground. Most bore no weapons, but there were some who carried bows and glaives of stone and wood.

Tiri came gracefully running over, with a handful of followers beside him. "What is His command, messenger of our Lord."

Larue answered: "He commands you to track down this evil which has followed you from your former home, and destroy it."

Tiri nodded: "As He commands. Ryia Nirag, send scouts out to look for it."

Nearby, on hand as always, Nirag replied to his king: "As you command, my hyrtyar. Trreon scarvir ity tris evir!"

Immediately, a score of scouts appeared from their hiding spot, running off to find those they sought. Nirag turned back to Tiri; "It is done, my hyrtyar. The scouts are on their way; they will find the evir soon."

"Good, Ryia," Tiri approved. "Gather the Dieferdar and wait for my order."

"Yes, my hyrtyar." Nirag turned to his men within earshot; "Let the horn sound to war!"

A loud horn was suddenly heard nearby.

Larue turned back to the king. "I will go back and wait for His calling."

"Farewell, my fela," Tiri said, warmly.

As Larue disappeared into a time portal which awaited nearby, again and again the horn could be heard, in short, loud bursts.

Before long, almost all of the Elves in sight were in the trees, now all armed and wearing their battle-armour. Women and men alike prepared to fight; only a handful remained behind, to keep watch over the children.

Shortly, a lone scout returned from his dispatch. He ran straight for the king and knelt before him. "My hyrtyar, we have located the evir – it is none other than Taroga Freyar."

Tiri winced at the name. "That is not good news, scout. Tell it to the time mage, quickly."

"Yes, my hyrtyar." The scout disappeared quickly out of sight, as Nirag took his place before the king.

"It seems our old enemy is back, my hyrtyar," he said.

"So it does, my fela," the king replied. "We almost didn't survive the last time we met. We must defeat it. May the Foresthoputye and the Time Lord be with us."

Nirag was optimistic; "We can win. The Dieferdar is ready."

"That may be," agreed Tiri, "but I fear the losses. How many will die?"

Nirag looked sombre. "Do you wish me to estimate, fela?"

Tiri shook his head; there was no point. "We have no time to waste. We must move out."

Nirag looked relieved. "Yes, my hyrtyar. I will wait for you."

As Nirag left, a young, tall and slender Elven man came running over to kneel by Tiri. Tiri addressed him first: "My enva, Jiri, this will be your first war, so just follow my lead."

Jiri nodded; "Yes, meati fari."

Tiri instructed: "Give me my aromiror."

Jiri went over to the armour stand. Taking an outfit of armour, he returned to hand it to his father, the king. Then, hurrying to another nearby stand, he proceeded to put on his own. When both men were dressed for battle, they were decorated with golden leaves; the patterns sewn into their suits showed their status.

"Do I look fine, meati fari?" Jiri asked.

Tiri laughed: "You look like a true vingara."

They came out of the trees, to the clearing of the forest path, where Nirag and the Dieferdar awaited them.

"Are you ready, my hyrtyar and vingara?" Nirag enquired.

Tiri replied: "I am, Ryia."

"I am ready," Jiri concurred. "I hope your training pays off."

Nirag smiled; "It will, Vingara. Let's move out. For glory and freedom!"

And, so started moving the caravan of 160 Elves and sixty Druids, behind the ryia, their hyrtyar and the vingara, all with glaives and bows in hand. The Druids were kept bound with ropes, as the Elves had to hasten them along, lest they keep stopping to hug all the trees and big stones, and such.

They reached the desert lands of Sandler. Nirag raised his hand to bring the army to a stop. "All hold!"

In front of them a whole camp was set up, for a large number of small, odious and malevolent green creatures. "Are those goblins?" asked Jiri.

Tiri nodded: "They are." Then, turning to the soldiers behind him, he called out: "For the future peace of the land, attack!"

An onslaught began; one-hundred elves shooting arrows all over the goblins' camp, taking the creatures by surprise. With sixty Elves, armed with glaives, around them, Tiri, Jiri and Nirag stood their ground, content to watch proceedings.

The goblins were jumping about and running in a panic, as one by one they were cut down. It wasn't long before the last remaining goblin was facing his death with a final, defiant hiss: "You will all die!"

"Stupid goblins," Nirag muttered at the spectacle. He then commanded: "Let's clear the bodies and set up camp here."

The Elves all put down their weapons and began moving the mass of dead goblins from the vicinity, releasing the Druids from their bonds to help. Then, with all of the corpses gone, they set up their tents. Their Elvish magic made light work of the task; with little more than the wave of a fingertip, the tents stood.

But, despite their hasty progress, all they could see was darkness ahead of them.

A little later, inside the hyrtyar's tent, Nirag was addressing his king: "My hyrtyar, what is the plan?"

Tiri was honest: "I don't know; all appears so dark."

"I think we should send out scouts, to locate where the evir was first seen and try to pick up his track," Jiri suggested.

Nirag agreed; "Sounds like a good plan, Vingara."

Tiri concurred, telling his ryia: "So, you have your orders. Now, leave us."

Nirag bowed his head. "Yes, my hyrtyar." Without hesitation, he departed the tent, leaving Tiri and Jiri alone.

Tiri turned to his son. "Mogein enva, soon we will leave on the comara."

Jiri answered: "Yes, Fari, we will go toward the road of peace."

Tiri looked forlorn. "I sense something darker than just him."

"I feel it too, meati fari."

Nirag suddenly came rushing back into the tent. "Hyrtyar, our scouts are back, and badly burnt! Something burns them when they touch the ground."

Tiri was wide-eyed. "What!? Lead the way. Jiri, come."

"Tyo, Fari."

As they were leaving, a group of ten Druids hurried into the tent.

"Grefyih hyrtyar, syoair wiynepo lyior. Tiri grefyih drenod, dyoy mentya foiy lotiy trreon," said the first.

"Tyo, Hyrtyar," added the second.

Tiri signalled the Druids to follow him, as he walked out of the tent, and they dropped into step behind Tiri, Jiri and Nirag.

On the outskirts of the camp, a tall and impressive, naked female was running about the place, tending to several badly burnt Elves. She was trying to treat them with herbs, as Tiri, Jiri and Nirag arrived with the entourage of Druids, who quickly set about helping.

"What horror is this?" Jiri uttered.

Tiri yelled to the woman: "Druor, what's going on here? How has this happened?"

The female, clearly irritated, turned around and marched defiantly over to Tiri. "What *happened* is that you didn't let my Druids check this area out first! The scouts ran into black mist!"

Nirag was furious; "Don't you speak—"

He was immediately interrupted by Tiri, who waved a hand to

quiet him. As Nirag instantly stopped talking, Tiri spoke calmly to the woman: "Silir, fela, the scouts should have picked this up, you know. I would have expected them to make the connection."

Silir picked up her robe, suddenly feeling exposed and disrespectful. She put it on before speaking. "I know, but still..." Then, she started to cry.

Tiri leaned in to her to comfort her. "I know what happened the last time. But, it won't happen again, I assure you, my fela."

Silir just remained silent, her mind wandering, as it flashed back to a recollection of events from her past. A group of Elves were marching along the dark, barren wasteland, covered by dead grass and ruined buildings. Suddenly, without warning, a number of them started to burn, their discomfort growing, until before long they were screaming in agony, their skin beginning to sear and blister. Then, they began to die, burning alive in torment. Before long, only a thick, black mist could be seen. One among them, Silir, just ran in a blind panic, screaming in horror, somehow untouched by the affliction. She could recall hearing only one word:

"Tearch."

Returning to the present, on the outskirts of the camp, Silir stood tall and faced Tiri, decisively; "There is little time. We need to cleanse the area."

Silir gathered the Druids in a circle and knelt with them, as they began to chant in some ancient Elven language, of which no one else present understood the meaning: *"Si Op Klo Ma Mits Ehs Vop Raq Xe Got Whisst Mits."*

As a thin, wispy, white mist emerged simultaneously from their mouths, they proceeded to strip down to nakedness, before the mist wrapped itself around them; the mist itself appeared to be filling with water. As it slowly crept outward, into the darkness, the Druids' chanting became ever more repetitive: *"Siria Misstior ooirow polonati jihreg pilatari. Yuto rimita rytuitor bcask gopron."*

After a very long time, watched over by any of the Elves still standing, the mist gradually began to dissipate into thin air. Finally, eventually, it was gone. The Druids collapsed in exhaustion; only Silir was still able to stand.

"It is done," she said; "the mist should not bother us anymore." She received no answer from anyone.

Suddenly, a deep booming voice was heard: "Freyar Tarogan!"

A huge, red creature appeared, some three-and-a-half metres tall. Alongside him, two-hundred similar, though slightly shorter of his kind appeared. And, behind them, an army of well over two-thousand goblins.

Tiri trembled at the sight of the terrifying Taroga Freyar. Yet, even through his fear, he gathered the Elves to battle. Most were already scared to death, but all stood ready.

What followed was no less than a horror of a battle. As the goblin army charged, a volley of arrows was let loose by the Elves – they killed or wounded all that they hit, but the storm advanced unimpeded.

The first wave of the enemy crashed into the line-formed Elves, their glaives at the ready. Many, from both sides, were killed at the moment of impact. But, the charge was unrelenting.

As all was looking bleak and darkness, Larue suddenly appeared at the scene. By his side stood eight others: time mages.

They positioned themselves in front of the Elves, and began their chanting: *"Let rain, thunder and earth shatter the enemies of the Lord of Time. Let the elements roar and thunder as they destroy!"*

Out of nowhere, holes began to pepper the ground. Lightning

and thunder poured down from above; rain followed. Swallowed up by the earth, and washed away by the tsunami of the elements, the Elves' enemies began to perish.

When the conjured storm finally subsided, there was no visible sign of it ever having occurred. Yet, in the end, only corpses were to be seen into the distance; fifteen-hundred enemies died as a result.

Now suddenly filled with renewed hope, the Elves charged into battle, their bows being discarded for stone knives, as they threw themselves into the raging battle. At their side, the time mages opened small portals all over, to suck the enemies into. Even the Druids now joined the fight, levitating roots and stones, to smash and crush their enemies to death. Elves, goblins and the red creatures alike fell, or disappeared into the portals.

By the time the battle was eventually over, only 140 Elves were standing; two of the Druids were dead, as was one of the time mages. Of their enemies, only Toroga Freyar still stood, waiting for someone to take him.

Nirag stepped forward, ready to do his duty. "It's been an honour to serve my hyrtyar." Then, before anyone could say a word to deter him, Nirag disappeared into the air, reappearing in front of the formidable enemy.

Even as started to cut and stab the red giant, Toroga Freyars was already attacking in frenzy, his claws making light work of ripping and tearing the poor Elf apart; the king could only watch his loyal servant die. But, even as Nirag lay slain, Toroga Freyar was himself dying, too, having been dealt a fatal blow, his stomach cut wide open, the guts hanging out of him.

In the aftermath of the battle, as a reward, I gave the Elves mounted creatures – deer the size of a full-blooded horse – to ride upon. Beautiful beasts known as elerats; a gift from me and their gods. The time mages took their fallen brother back to the Time Tower, to send him off on his way, while the Elves buried their dead underneath new trees they planted, before returning home to mourn their losses.

Two-hundred years would pass before the race of Elves would be called to arms once again. But, that is a story for another time; for now, we will say our goodbyes to them, until the next time...

Chapter Two

The Humans

Now I tell another story of the people of this land: that of how Humans came to be.

A hundred years had passed since the just-narrated event; by now the Elves were prospering, their numbers having boomed to well over one-thousand. I had already begun to work on creating Humans, in the same way I made my time mages: using the magic of time. I took stone-clay earth and water, and shaped the first twenty Humans.

I gave the males the names Wilson Eradon, Will Seros, Kent Skrap, Ben Bent, Woody Woodhawk, Ulf Sieg, Willfred Bellow, Fred Iggos, Simon Simonsen and Jesper Japer. The females I named Marry Eradon, Mimi Seros, Tilda Sharp, Ira Bent, Winny Woodhawk, Marie Seig, Nannar Bellow, AnnMarie Iggos, Juliet Simonsen and Lisbet Japer – their brides, of course. I then proceeded to make several other smaller families and the like, as well as horses which, though strong, steady and calm, were the size of a full-blood pedigree.

They made their city in the grassland of Grarss's southern border, naming it Grassiak. It resembled a towering, middle-ages settlement, the vast city spanned by two high, thick walls: one inner wall and one outer, with large, impenetrable gates at each. The outer circle of the city was where the poor quarters were situated, for the many poor people in the east; farms and allotments made up much of the outer ring's west side.

The inner circle of the city comprised the commons and craft area to the east, with the noble area to the west. In the centre of the city was a hill, on the top of which sat the grand manor in which the king lived, itself guarded by another, smaller perimeter wall and gate. Nearby was also the cathedral, which I built for their god.

I put into the Humans' mind the knowledge to craft and fight, but I kept this knowledge firmly no later than what you would know as of the fifteenth century; they would have no knowledge of gunpowder, as I considered this an unfair advantage over other races. Their knowledge of cloth I took from a later era, equivalent to Victorian times on Earth, while their medical knowledge was from the modern age. I made sure that men and women alike would consider themselves equal, and would draw their knowledge from a wide scene.

After half a century had passed, I started to toy with them, creating ten smaller noble houses: Solmon, Medicar, Silri, Solrup, Konshap, Jarg, Centrak, Brest, Joggok and Gelgirk.

From the very beginning, I gave them a god to worship which was other than myself: Lightors, the god of light and life itself. I created an order of priests to follow him, which I named "The Order of Torsfor".

After those first fifty years passed, since I had made and shaped them, I then left them to grow on their own, building their armies, and so on. During that time, a time mage messenger named Larus visited them often, and prayed to me on their behalf.

When two-hundred years had passed since what I came to name "The Battle of Darkness", I allowed Larue to send a message to the Elves, requesting that they meet with the Humans on the border of Rroker – the rocky, mountainous terrain between Grarss and the Golden Forest – in a hut which I made for the purpose. In turn, Larus would make the same request of the Humans.

And so, Tiri, the king of the Elves, and Wike Sharp, the current king of the Humans – the latter a tall man, some two metres in height, and broad with muscles clearly showing – would meet. The account which follows is what happened, and then what subsequently followed, in that late summer...

17

On the road from Grarss to Rroker.

Wike was riding along the rocky terrain, along with Turun and a handful of high guards on horses, a foot army, and a high priest known as Marok. All were armoured up in plate, or brigandine for the poor army, while white plate armour was worn by the High Guard.

Captain Peter asked, curiously: "My king, is there a reason we are meeting with these so-called Elves?"

Turun skulked at him: "Don't question your king's actions, Captain."

Wike intervened: "Easy, my wife, I understand the good captain's concerns. Let me answer you, Captain: it is because Larus said so. I trust him with my life, as did my father and my grandfather before that. He has helped us a lot over the years, and he never asks for anything in return. So, of course I do this, if he asks me to."

Peter nodded, sheepishly: "Of course, my king. I apologize. I am just not particularly trusting of them."

"I understand," said Wike, "but this might be a good opportunity to establish allies, in case of times of battle."

"I agree," Marok interjected. "Plus, it is also a chance to discuss their religion, and to share our own."

Wike smiled; "Always short and on point, Marok."

"I do aim to please, my king."

They chuckled. Their journey continued.

*

At around the same time, over by the way from the Golden Forest to Rroker, Tiri and Jiri were riding forth, with their entourage and twenty Elves on foot, silently; only the hooves of the animals were to be heard.

Silir had been brought for the trip, her arms bound to Tiri's mount, as she struggled against them. "I need to go and hug those rocks; so beautiful."

"Silence!" Tiri barked. "I don't want to hear another complaint from you. The only reason I brought you along is because you are our spiritual leader. Got it?"

Silir only mumbled, angrily.

Ryia Tirias spoke: "My hyrtyar, how long until we get there?"

Tiri replied: "Eager to meet the Humans?"

"Aren't you, my hyrtyar? Wasn't it foretold, two-hundred years ago, that we would meet them?"

"Yes," said Tiri, "but I admit I am a little apprehensive of how they will respond to us."

"Well, I think this is a great opportunity," said Jiri. "And, who knows, maybe we can create a crossbreed." Jiri chuckled at his own comment.

Tiri perused. "Well, I'm open to it. But, only time will tell."

A few days later, the Humans and the Elves met in front of the time hut, all eyeing one another cautiously.

The tension dissipated a little when Larus and Larue appeared between them.

Larus addressed the group leaders: "Please, let your party stay out here in my care, and follow my dear Larue inside. Only the most important may come along."

"Very well," said Tiri; "Jiri and Silir will follow me."

Tiri and Jiri dismounted and unbound Silir, keeping a careful hold of her as she dismounted the horse. She then followed her king inside. Wike Turun and Marok were next, before Larue followed them in. Their respective entourages settled down to wait.

Inside the time hut, Tiri, Jiri and Silir sat down on one side of the large, long table, while Wike Turun and Marok sat on the other.

Larue took a seat at one end of the table. He spoke first: "You have been gathered here today so that your two races can explore ways to co-exist, and in the future, hopefully, be allies in defending these lands. Please state your names and titles, in the langue of time."

"I'll start," Tiri said; "my name is Tiri, King of the Elves." He stood and bowed, before sitting down again.

Jiri stood then to speak. "My name is Jiri, Prince of the Elves." He, too, bowed then sat down.

Silir stood next. She had neglected to fasten her robes, and they fell as she stood; she stood before them naked. Indifferently, she addressed them: "My name is Silir, High Druid of the Elves; their spiritual leader." Then, she simply sat down and again donned her robes.

As the shock of seeing the naked Elf began to wear off amongst the Humans, Wike stood up in his armour and said: "My name is Wike, King of the Humans."

After Wike took a brief bow and sat down, Turun stood next, also in her armour. "My name is Turun, wife of Wike and Queen of the Humans." Turun sat back down after bowing.

Marok was next: "My name is Marok, High Priest of the Humans and representative of our spiritual leader, Angel Mariaka."

Larue waited patiently for the last of the introductions, before taking the reins again. "Now that is in order, let's talk about our concerns and the like."

So, the talks began, bouncing back and forth between the two kings, the prince and a queen. When they were finally done, after many hours had passed, Marok and Silir began to talk between themselves, about religion and culture. When all was done, a treaty was put forth by Larue and signed by both parties.

Larue concluded the talks. "It is agreed, then: a trade route will be made between your two lands, which will be split into halves. One side will be guarded by Elves, the other by Humans. Additionally, you will enter into an alliance.

"Each of your species will have the right to choose which religion and path they follow, and you will each allow priests or Druids of each other's race to bring mission to your main city, and preach about their religion. Am I correct in all that I have reiterated?"

All nodded their heads in agreement, and Larue knelt in prayer, while the rest looked on.

At the very same moment, I sent a message to Larue. The corrupt mage – or that to which I more accurately refer as a "time corruption mage" – was known to me as Miller. I was aware that he had captured many goblins and twisted them with magic, transforming them into two-and-half-metre, dark-green brutes: Orcs. Orcs were notoriously low on intelligence, and barely able to converse better than a Human child, but they were strong enough to break stones apart with their bare hands.

However, most interesting about my observations was that I saw signs of dissent; some of those being held captive seemed somewhat reluctant to do as he commanded. I foresaw that these rebellious individuals may prove useful to us in the future.

I sent all of this information to Larue to relay, whilst still in his meeting.

Back at the hut, Larue rose to his feet and relayed the message from his Lord.

The others looked on, and listened to his words with surprise. They were further shocked when Larue told them: "I must ask you to find this army and take it out, before it's too late. Rescue those who are held captive against their will and grant them amnesty; allow them to settle, despite the hatred and mistrust which they will encounter from your people."

Wike sneered: "Why can we not just kill them?"

Larue told him: "As I have already said, they are deemed to be useful in the future by my Lord. Please do as I ask, for the sake of peace."

Tiri nodded. "I will comply. I will gather what I can and send scouts to find this warmonger. I suspect he can be found somewhere deep in Sandler, though I have no knowledge of this."

"Fine," Wike agreed, "then I will gather my army, the noble High Guard and as many priests, supplies and people as I can. We will meet in your city in seventy days' time."

Tiri nodded his agreement. "Very well. May the forest gods guide you to them."

Wike returned: "And, may Lightors do the same for you."

All rose and bowed, before leaving.

Ten days later, in the Human capital of Grassiak.

By the time Wike returned from the meeting, along with Turun, Marok and Captain Peter, a scout had already gone ahead of them to prepare, and now the soldiers, priests and civilian servants were rushing about the place, getting packed and preparing horses, ready to set out at a moment's notice.

As they came to a weary halt, a woman came hurrying toward them, kneeling as they readied to dismount.

"Excuse me, my king, may I speak a word from my master, the great inventor, Ivan."

Wike grumpily snapped: "Speak quickly. I am tired after my journey."

Lise replied: "Of course, my king. My master has just found a solution to the issues with our weapons; he believes he may know more about them now. He wishes to see you as soon as possible."

"Actually, that sounds interesting," Wike mused. "I will see him at once. Captain, order the troops to stable the horses and supplies. And find my squire and that of my wife, to take our horses to the royal stables, then follow behind us."

Peter nodded respectfully: "Yes, my king. Troops, get the horses and supplies to the stables, and find the king and queen's squires to take their horses to the royal stables."

The soldiers complied quickly, as Peter, Wike and Turun dismounted. Shortly after, a boy around sixteen years old, and a girl of the same age, came to take Wike and Turun's horses, leading them off. Wike, Turun and Peter followed Lise to the great inventor's house.

Lise led them down a street of average status, some of the dwellings rough, others well-kempt. They followed her into the largest of them all.

Inside, they found a man who looked very old, with almost no hair, other than a few grey tots. He wore strange spectacles and a grey robe. He appeared to be working on some sort of handheld projectile weapon, and not to have seen them enter.

Wiki interrupted him, loudly: "What is so important you need to discuss it with your king, Ivan?"

Ivan almost jumped from his chair, then relaxed as he faced his company. "My king, I did not expect you so readily; I fancied you too tired from your journey. I will quickly get to the point."

He spoke in a high-pitched tone, which seemed to gradually increase with excitement as he picked up the new weapon from his workbench. "As you are aware, bows and crossbows have advantages and disadvantages. However, I believe I have found a solution to the latter. By combining the crossbow with the bow, and adding a stock with a powerful spring mechanism, which allows us to quickly slide to load, we can shoot bolts faster, more precisely and farther than before. I can produce great numbers of them very quickly, if needed. So far, my tests have yielded a range of four-hundred metres, without any loss of accuracy. I call it a 'spring-loaded bow'."

"Interesting," Wike uttered. "Captain, proceed to test this weapon."

"As you command, my king," Peter replied.

"You may use the target range I have set up in the backyard," Ivan said, leading them outside. They walked into a sizeable backyard, to see a shooting target pinned onto a hay bale at the far end, almost a hundred feet away.

Peter took the spring-loaded bow from the inventor, loading a long, thick iron bolt into it. Without so much as a strain, he pulled the handle on the side of the weapon's stock, cocking the bowstring. Once done, he shouldered the weapon as instructed by Ivan, pointed at the target and fired.

The projectile was in the air for no more than a second, before it penetrated the target, emerging from the rear and striking the solid clay wall behind, where it got stuck fast. They cheered and clapped, as Ivan jovially bowed.

"Impressive," Peter grinned. "No recoil, yet more powerful than any weapon I have ever seen."

Ivan bowed again. "Thank you. If my king wishes for more of these weapons, I will require to take ownership of all crossbows and bowstrings we have available, so that I may modify them to use this system. I can convert all weapons within thirty days, if I am afforded help to do so."

Wike didn't hesitate. "I will make sure that you get them, and I will send engineers down here to help out and to learn this craft. The blacksmiths will proceed to work on this project as fast as they are able. All will be paid for by the Crown."

Ivan was gleeful. "I thank you, my king; you do me a great honour."

Wike turned to Peter: "Captain, make sure this happens. You may leave my service immediately once we reach the castle, and proceed with the instruction."

Peter nodded. "As my king commands."

Feeling positive, they then left Ivan and Lise to their work.

At the king's manor.

Immediately as Wike and Turun said their goodbyes to Peter and entered the manor, they were accosted by an eight-year-old girl, jumping ecstatically into their arms, her governess waiting dutifully nearby.

"Mamma! Pappi!" squealed Princess Scarlet. "You are back!"

Wike and Turun both knelt down to hug their daughter, as Nanny Poppin now approached with a smile. "Now, calm down, girl. Allow them to get out of their armour and relax before you climb all over them."

Wike smiled. "It's alright, Poppin. I've missed my baby girl."

After allowing the family a few moments to reunite, out of one of the rooms a tall, broad and muscular young woman appeared, with a longsword hanging at her side. She addressed the princess: "It's time for training, young lady, if you want to be as strong as your daddy."

Clearly not in the mood for her lesson, Scarlet pouted: "Don't want to! You're mean!"

The young woman, meanwhile, was not in the mood for the girl's tantrums. She simply walked over, took Scarlet by the arm and dragged her away. All the while, Scarlet screamed for her pappi.

Wike shook his head. "Do as High Captain Iris says, baby. Maybe I will have a treat for you later – if you behave."

Scarlet immediately calmed down and, though still not happy, she followed Iris without further complaint.

Turun sneered at her husband. "You're making her a spoiled brat. You know that, darling?"

Wike looked sheepish. "I know, but she will learn."

Thankfully, the young squires shortly returned from the royal stable, following Wike and Turun to the armoury, so they could finally get out of their armour.

Wike and Turun came walking into the throne room, clad in their blue and red cloth. They sat beside each other, at the end of a large, stone table.

As soon as they were seated, the doors were opened by two high guards holding halberds, and Scarlet came running in, with her hand and head bandaged, crying for her pappi. Wike immediately took her onto his lap as she approached.

Scarlet cried: "Iris hurt me, Pappi."

Wike replied: "I know, sweetie. It is her job to hurt you; to train you, until you become a good fighter."

Turun looked over at the two of them. "She reminds me of you as a child, dear."

Still comforting his little girl, Wike answered: "Don't remind me."

Iris came into the throne room, opening the doors for herself. She bowed upon reaching them.

"How is my girl faring in training, High Captain?" Wike asked her.

"My king, she is getting better as the days go by. Over the years, though, she will be much better if she toughens up and stops whining about the pain – with all due respect, of course."

Wike smiled, dismissively; "I understand completely, High Captain."

He faced his daughter, who looked up at her pappi, her face covered in tears; "Listen to me, baby girl: if you don't start to act like a warrior princess – worthy to one day take the throne – the people will rebel and they will disgrace you, because they know you cannot fight. I won't always be there for you."

"Yes, Pappi."

"Good. Now, go with Iris and help her with her duties. You are her page, and will one day be her squire; one must be humble before they can lead. Iris, go by the kitchen and get a cookie for her."

Iris nodded. "Yes, my king."

Scarlet jumped down from her father's lap, happier now, and followed Iris out of the room.

Passing them through the doorway was Herald Harry. He approached the table and bowed before them. "My king, my queen, do you wish for a meal to be brought to you following your journey, or do you wish to rest for tonight's gathering?"

Turun replied: "We wish to be escorted to our room, and to rest for tonight's gathering."

Wike agreed: "Yes, indeed. But, please also bring a small meal to our room."

Harry bowed; "It shall be done." Then, he clapped twice, summoning four high guards to escort Wike and Turun out of the room. As they left, Harry followed for a distance, then turned off toward the kitchen.

Later that evening, in the throne room, a number of people had gathered: nobles from all of the existing orders. From Negpol (negotiation and politics) was their leader, High Justice Imark; representing Armyr (war and army management) was their own leader, Commandor Arlerk; the order for holy war and holy life, Torsfor, was represented by its leader, Angel Mariaka; and Higbles (the order of the High Guard and the nobles) was led by High Captain Irma.

The doors swung open as Wike and Turun entered, flanked by four high guards. Instantly, word burst from the crowd: "All hail the king and queen! Lightors watch over them and prolong their life!"

They made their way to their respective thrones and sat down. They were dressed in their finest cloth, as were most present.

Harry stood in front of them and started to shout: "Order in the throne room. Let this meeting begin!" As silence fell, Harry spoke up again: "We are gathered here today to discuss a war effort, against a corrupt time mage, who has twisted the goblins into tall monsters we now know to be Orcs. We are not to kill them, but instead to banish them; we will allow the time mages to handle any further. We have allied ourselves with the Elves, and both pledged to eradicate this evil before it destroys us all."

A tall, slim, though densely-muscled young woman approached the throne, bowing before she spoke to Harry: "And, why should we do that? Orcs are monsters; they should be destroyed. I demand this in the name of Lightors."

As the crowd slowly started to clap her words, Wike stood up, holding a palm toward Harry, who allowed him to take over the oration. The crowd became silent, as their king addressed them: "I understand your concerns, Angel Mariaka. The fact is that, if we do this, we gain more power, and perhaps future allies; we may yet be here for centuries to come. But, more importantly, we will have the allegiance of the time mages. You must understand that our god only co-exists with the Time Lord himself. We are not a racist species; we must accept others for who they are."

Mariaka was about to grumble but, as she turned away, the crowd was already starting to cheer and clap their king.

Irma stood next, raising a hand for permission to speak. Harry nodded to her. Irma asked: "My king, my queen, since – according to my knowledge of the situation – you appear intent on moving most of our army and High Guard, I respectfully ask how many enemies we are to expect."

Turun stood to answer the question: "We expect over a hundred Orcs, plus a corrupt time mage with unknown powers."

Irma nodded her gratitude, before bowing and stepping back into the crowd.

Now, it was Arlerk's turn to step forward and bow, before speaking: "Might I suggest contacting the time mages for their aid, due to our own lack of any magical defence?"

Wike agreed: "An excellent idea. Harold, send a messenger right away."

Harry nodded; "As you command, my king." He hurried to fetch a page, penning a quick letter, before sending it off with the boy.

Arlerk took a step back, clearly satisfied with the decisive answer and response to his suggestion.

An old man, crouched over, now stepped forward to speak: High Justice Imark. "My king, my queen, may I suggest that we of the Order of Negotiation and Politics cooperate with the time mages and, when the time is right, make an alliance with these Orcs? If they are correct, the Orcs could prove useful if tamed, and may even come to gain an understanding of us."

Wike nodded. "I agree. However, don't yield too much, or forsake us, just to gain an alliance; it must be on mutual grounds, like that between us and the Elves."

"As you command, my king," Imark bowed, before stepping back away.

Wike stood to address the crowd, and they gave him their full attention. "I know that we should be discussing where and how many scouts should be sent, but I will in fact leave this task to the Elves: they know more about the land than we do, and I would rather not lose any of ours mapping the area. For the next thirty days, instead, we gather supplies and arm our forces; we shall move out within forty, to reach the Elven city in plenty of time. Do we all agree on this?"

The crowd called out in unison: "We are with you, my king; my queen!"

As the court-session closed, and the people start to clear the room, many were whispering to each other on the way out. Soon, only one remained in the company of the king and queen. Wike looked at her. "Is something wrong, High Captain?"

Iris looked at him for a moment, before saying: "My king, if I may speak freely?"

Wike nodded: "Of course. I can't have my high captain worried."

"Thank you, my king. My concern is Angel Mariaka; she seems obsessed with wiping out the Orcs. Might I advise not assigning her any command post, and to leave this task to myself or Captain Peter? I am not entirely sure of the intentions of the holy order, my king."

Wike sighed. "I understand your concern, High Captain, and I share it with you. However, I will leave her to command her troops, though she will do so under your guidance; no orders will be issued without your approval.

"But, I most burden you with another task: that of keeping Scarlet safe. I have decided I would like her to attend; she needs to experience the battlefield."

"Thank you, my king," said Iris. "Yes, it is time she learnt what it means to kill another, and to live the reality of battle – the sounds; the smells – even if I have to drag her there."

At this, Turun turned her attention toward Iris. "I bet you will need to drag her with you, as well; she isn't the keenest to learn – I hope she will soon. You have my blessing to do whatever is needed to toughen her up. She might hate you later, but she will thank you for making her a survivor."

Iris nodded, bowing before she took her leave, just as new high guards came on shift to replace those departing. They bowed their heads toward Iris, who returned the gesture, then signalled the six in situ to follow her out, in two lines of three behind her.

Shortly after, Wike and Turun would leave court, followed by their own lines of guards.

The personal scribe of King Wike Williams wrote, in his first report of the time year 25560:

> "My ledge and his queen spent most of the days checking the supplies and forces at their disposal. Arguments came, mostly from Torsfor, for leaving High Guard and the regular army in overall command.
>
> "They had to change their bows and crossbows for the new spring-loaded bow, but when they saw how deadly they were, and how much

more precise than anything they had ever seen, they did so happily. Morale became so high that a hundred more men joined within ten days, and were given postings in just twenty days. Mercenaries were hired as well, to increase the number of our fighting forces.

"We set out on an early-October morning."

Thirty days after holding court, the battle-party stood at the southern gate of Grassiak, looking out across Grarss.

Wike, Turun, Iris and Peter sat on their horses, ready to move out, alongside Angel and Arlerk. Behind them was an army of more than three-hundred Humans, from all corners of the capital, high guards and the forces of the Order of Torsfor.

Behind the troops, more than two-hundred civilians followed: squires, servants, whores and many others needed for the camps. With them were priests of Lightors, in their discernible yellow and white robes. High guards and the High Cavalry brought up the rear, comprising nearly two-hundred noblemen and women.

There was no sign of the time mages, yet. Not willing to wait any longer, Wike gave the signal for the mass of forces to move out. The sound of boots and hooves, alongside that of goat horns and drums, was deafening as they departed.

*

Into the journey, Wike Williams reported:

"The days go by quickly. We stop, we hunt and we camp. I have had to continually listen to the princess complaining about how badly Iris treats her – hopefully, one day, she will grow up. Arguments and fights occasionally break out amongst the men, and are stopped by the leaders. It is not easy on the road, but they are thankfully quiet, until we reach the edge of the Elven Forest."

At the southern edge of the Golden Forest, the forces stopped, taking a break before entering the Elves' domain.

They had barely even dismounted, when arrows were suddenly hurtling toward them; many of the party were hit straight away. The arrows didn't appear to be Elven in design.

A large party of bandits appeared, their bows at the ready, as they yelled out: "Death to the false people!"

Wike quickly leapt to his feet alongside Turun, and both drew their longswords, while ten of the high guards scrambled to form a protective ring around them, clad in their white plate armour and surcoats – five were bearing halberds and five swords and shields.

The priests rushed to tend to the wounded, who were screaming out as they bled. Iris and Angel charged head-on into the bandits, as a volley of covering bolts flew overhead; a large number of the bandits dropped, dead or wounded, as others ran to take cover behind the trees. Those who did so, however, were quickly overrun, and surprised by the ferocity of Iris and Angel's attack; the two cut down the retreaters mercilessly as they tried to flee. The melee was over in mere moments.

Peter returned with one of the fleeing bandits his captive, after whom he had rode off in pursuit.

"Nice one, Captain," Wike approved. "Bring him here so we can talk."

Peter dragged the bandit to his feet, then shoved him over to face Wike. The bandit put up something of a fight, as he was pulled by the rope around his torso. Peter tossed him to the ground, as the high guards quickly trained their weapons on him.

Wike told the bandit: "Tell me who you are working with, and I will execute you quickly."

"I will never talk to a false leader!" the bandit hissed, spitting in Wike's face.

Iris walked up behind the bandit and kicked him brutally in the back. With a yelp, he dropped to the ground.

"Thank you, High Captain," Wike said to her. "Now, again, tell me what I want to know, or I will make the next ten minutes of your life a living hell."

The bandit smirked. "Go eat slug, you false king of shit."

Wike looked at him, coldly, for a few moments. "Fine. Captain Peter, please drag this fool aside and deal with him."

Peter, still clutching the rope, mounted his horse, then began a steady pace, a little way into the forest. He was indifferent when the bandit fell, to continue the journey dragged across the rough ground.

After watching them leave, Iris turned to face Princess Scarlet, whose face was pale. "Come with me," she said.

Scarlet's immediate belief was that it was the intention of her guardian to shield her from the sounds of what Captain Peter was about to do. That was, however, until the high captain informed the child of her duty to tend the wounded troops – and to dispatch the more gravely injured with a dagger across the throat. Scarlet started to cry and struggle, resisting with all of her strength, but Iris's resolve was stronger still, as she dragged the girl off to kill men.

For the next ten minutes, the party were sombre and quiet; the only sounds to be heard were the bandit's distant screams of agony, and his begging for mercy.

After what felt like an age, Peter returned; he was alone, his armour covered in blood. He rode over toward Wike and whispered something into his ear.

Wike nodded. "I will deal with this later," he said, before giving the order for the group to continue: "Move out!"

And, so the gathered forces proceeded into the Golden Forest, toward the Elven city.

They reached the Elven city ten days later.

The gathered Human forces stopped shortly before the entrance to the city, where Wike signalled for them to wait, as he, Turun and Iris rode up to the gate, alongside Angel. At the entrance, several Elves were waiting, some with bows and glaives in hand, clearly still wary of the Humans.

The tension eased a little when Hyr Tiri appeared, walking gracefully, with Jiri in tow.

"Hir humir," spoke Tiri. "I greet you, King of Humans, and I greet your forces. Welcome to Earasira, our city and home. You are the first outsiders ever to visit here, and hopefully the first of many to behold our lovely city."

Wike nodded. "It is good to be among allies, if trust is yet not earned – but, it soon will be, for a nation can't grow without it, nor can it be called one."

Tiri concurred: "True words, indeed. Come. We will eat as we discuss a plan of battle. Your people can camp over in the clearing, nearby. Jiri, please show them the way."

"Tyo, Fari," Jiri nodded, leading out to show the party where to camp.

After dismounting and passing their horses to the squires who came running to attend, Wike, Turun, Iris and Angel followed. They noted with interest, as they observed naked Druids hugging trees, and Elves working with meat skin and tools they had never seen before, for what appeared a wide range of trades. Most of the crafts were being carried out on the ground, though Elves could also be seen working in the hollowed-out trees which were their homes. Tiri ascended a staircase up the side of the most giant tree, which promised an even grander home inside; he waited at the top for them to join him.

Inside the home of King of Elves, they found a throne made of roots and branches, twisted and woven by Elven magic. Before it was a grand table, conjured from a large, shining stone, its chairs crafted of twisted roots. The table was easily big enough to accommodate twenty people.

"Please, sit," Tiri invited. "Food and drinks will soon be served."

Shortly after they had made themselves comfortable, Jiri entered, with Arlerk and Silir in tow. Tiri and Wike were seated at one end, with Jiri sitting opposite Iris, then Angel and Arlerk. The Humans all still wore battle dress.

Ryia Tirias entered soon after, himself clad in armour. "I apologize: I saw the ambush you encountered while out scouting earlier. I will make sure there is a patrol at every given moment now, King of Humans."

Wike replied: "No bother; we can manage – but I thank you for doing so."

Elven servants entered, with bottles of fine wine, both red and white. One poured each diner a glass of their preference, into a beautiful glass cup being held by another. There were many servants, both male and female, young and slightly older. After placing the bottles onto a wooden tray, on the table to the side, the servants left through a side door.

The party each took a sip for politeness, before Tiri spoke: "Ryia, please report what our scouts have so far spotted."

"Tyo mogein, Hyr." Tirias turned to face the guests. "Our scouts have spotted a strange hole in the sand, in the centre of Sandler. We spotted a number of Orcs guarding it, and very likely more inside, though that is unknown. We have also spotted something worse: Corrupted Elves ."

The Humans looked unfamiliarly at Tirias, not aware of the basis of his concern. Wike asked: "What are Corrupted Elves ?"

Tiri answered: "The same as us, really, but they have sold their souls and their loyalty to those from whom we fled: the Efor empire... 'demons', I believe you Humans would call them. The Corrupted Elves are twisted, and will do their masters' bidding without any words of question."

"That confirms our fears, then."

They all turned to face the voice, to see that Larue and Larus had appeared in the door. Larus said: "Please excuse us for being late."

Tiri replied: "Please don't worry; I'm sure you have much to do. Take a seat and something to drink. Food shall be served shortly."

Larue and Larus sat, pouring themselves a glass of white wine each. Then, Larue explained: "Our mages found the remnants of a portal, in Sedrak, north of Sandler. It is very likely that the Corrupted Elves enter from there. The western border of the Golden Forest, near Sandler, has grown dark and deadened of late."

Tiri nodded; "I know of this. I have lost Elves scouting there. The arrows which killed them made us suspect Corrupted Elves , but we had no solid evidence, until now."

Wike said, wryly: "Just great. Then, we will have a good fight on our hands."

Tiri was more upbeat; "Combined, we should have enough forces to deal with this."

"Yes, indeed," Larue agreed. "We brought six mages along with us, so we should be fine."

Silir now intervened: "My Druids will handle the Corrupted Elves ' dark, twisted magic."

Wike was yet wary. "I still worry about what we will face, and the unknown is never good. I can't promise my regular army won't turn tail and run, but the orders of Torsfor and the High Guard will fight to the end."

Arlerk saw an opportunity to gloat: "My first regiment will never turn and retreat, or I will have their heads! And, that counts for Captain Peters' second regiment; they know what he will do to them if they disobey orders!"

"I expect nothing less from such an elite army."

Tiri listened to the exchange. "It's good to know that at least some of your so-called army has guts!"

Larue intervened, lest this be misinterpreted as a slight, as which it was not intended: "Humans have a natural instinct to flee, when fear takes them. But, I trust King Wike to instil in his troops the morale to fight for each other."

Turun leaned across and said, softly: "My dear husband usually leaves that part to me."

Although the Elves were not sure if this was a serious comment or a humorous one, Wike simply nodded.

It wasn't long before the servants returned, carrying lots of food, including deer steaks and fresh salad, concocted of all that the forest provided. The meat was put on the table and carved to perfect thickness, as the servants served it, beautifully arranged on the plate, on a bed of crushed nuts with a salad side.

Tiri's mouth watered. "Let's concentrate on eating and finish this conversation after."

No one argued. They all started to dig in, the moment the plates were put before them, their fine wooden cutlery already waiting, on a small towel to clean hands and mouths. They mostly ate silently, some quietly making casual small-talk. Angel and Silir were conversing about religion, and comparing their own, while Wike and Tiri chatted about the hardships of ruling;

Tirias, Arlerk and Jiri chatted about army life and warfare tactics. Larue and Larus were content to just sit, eat, drink and listen to the others. They took their time to enjoy the meal, though still it passed; soon they were done eating, and the dishes were taken away.

Instantly, they returned to the matter at hand.

"So, how should we organize our troops?" Tiri enquired.

"I suggest this," Wike replied: "I position my regular army at the front, armed with swords, axes and maces; they will be supported by the mercenaries, and covered from behind by my High Guard, with their halberds and longswords. Behind the front I propose we position Angel and her holy army, with the priests forming a third line, followed by the Druids – all covered by the Elven archers. I will be with the Elven archers, with our entire arsenal of spring-loaded bows, since we have many more of them. I will be positioned in the middle of the troops, along with my queen, protected by a ring of High Guard around us – you and your son will stand alongside us there, with your glaives. On the flanks, Iris will lead the mounted High Guard and Captain Peters' second regiment, mounted infantry, supported by mercenaries on horseback. The time mages will focus on the magic of the corrupt one, while the Druids should focus the Dark Elven magic."

Having listened intently, Larue concurred with the strategy: "Very well. We will position ourselves as required."

Tiri agreed: "A solid plan, indeed, using our strengths to support our weak points. I approve it."

"Good," Silir intervened, though with a word of caution: "but, be aware that they will try to sneak inside our ranks."

Angel scoffed: "Let them; my priest will reveal the darkness around them."

"I will place my company in front, to promote morale,"

suggested Arlerk.

Tiri was satisfied with all that he had heard. "So, this settles our plan, yes?"

Wike nodded; "It does. Let's retire for the night and brief our troops tomorrow morning."

"Sounds good."

With that, they all stood and afforded each other a courteous bow, before retiring for the night.

Early the next morning, in their camp, the Human forces stood ready, waiting to move out.

Wike was ready for battle, with Turun alongside him. Arlerk and Angel were nearby, and Iris was mounted, with a not-at-all-happy-looking Scarlet on a horse by her side.

The entire army stood before Wike in anticipation, waiting for him to speak. Finally, he was ready.

"My people – my fellow men and women of the Human kingdom – we stand united today with the Elves, to banish the evil which threatens to tear our land apart. We will not allow that to happen! We will stand in the way of this evil, and display our will, and our strength in numbers. We will show that we do not back down, until we are victorious!

"So, walk and ride forth. Show me that my words are true. Show me what I already know: that we will win!"

The forces cheered their king loudly, and he allowed the moment to linger, before they began their ride out to meet the Elves.

At the same moment, in the Elven city of Earasira...

The Elves' Dieferdar stood at the ready, as Tiri and Jiri were before them, with Silir and Tirias at their side.

Tiri addressed his army: "Eflar staciv umira apre shiume humir, wiyenpo Torein ruhir togrer arti tris evir. Topri darari humir. Fram Foresthoputye!"

The Dieferdar cheered their king heartily, as they too began the move out to unite with the Humans.

The Elves met up with the Human forces at the northern edge of the Golden Forest, in preparation to move onward on their journey.

For the Elves, it was a slow trip, but they learnt much about the Humans on the way. Some were even starting to befriend (and, dare say, even flirt) with each another. Even so, all knew the jollity wouldn't last for long.

The king's scribe wrote, in his second report of the time year 25560:

"We have now travelled for more than three weeks, across the hot, dry sand. The Elves are a big help in finding water sources, as well as food. Love has blossomed between Elves and men, though I believe nothing has of yet been consummated, their flirtations more playful in nature! We all know that war will take this humour from us in the blink of an eye, but it is clear to see that our people have the capability and the desire to co-exist with each other. Perhaps half-breeds might come into being in the future! Who knows?

"I have been training alongside the men, as I requested to stay near the king during the battle, to record all on paper. I know I need to be ready to defend myself, carrying out this dangerous task, yet I am proud to take such action for my king; I live only to serve.

"The caravan has finally come to a stop now, as we build camp and prepare for battle. It is an anxious time. People pray to their gods; those Humans who are able write their farewell letters to loved ones; while the

Elves allow the Druids to prepare their return to the earth and the trees. Prayers are conducted by Druids, time mages and Lightors priests in conjunction; many gather for this, to gain courage and comfort from their respective religion before battle. We have set up the battleground on a flat, sandy area not far from the camp. It is two days since we arrived, and troops have already been sent to their positions. The enemy is not far away now. It is time.

"I hereby end this report.

"Signed by royal scribe,

"William Anark."

Somewhere in central Sandler...

Troops stood tall and strong; formations were being made.

Iris and Peter were posted on the flanks of the battlefield, with the cavalry. Arlerk and Angel were the front lines.

In the middle were Wike and Turun, along with their loyal and brave scribe, William. Beside them were Jiri and Tiri, within a shield of High Guard and Elves bearing glaives. Behind them, Elves and men stood side-by-side, with bows at the ready.

Druids, priests and mages mixed with the ranks.

In front of the allied mass stood their enemy: an army of nearly five-hundred Orcs; four-hundred Corrupted Elves ; and, six-hundred soldiers of Efors – tall, red creatures, between three and five metres in height, with long tails, pointed horns and Elf-like hands. All were armed, with daggers, bows, swords, maces, axes and shields; some carried longswords and others large, two-handed axes or maces. Most of the Orcs and Efors soldiers wore little more than brigandine-type armour, of both leather and iron; some wore none.

In the middle of the horde stood Miller. He wore a dark-red and black cloth robe; his face was hidden.

The two armies faced each other. Last minute prayers were carried out, and both sides prepared for battle.

Larue stepped out onto the battlefield, to address Miller; he used time magic to project his voice. "Miller, formerly of the Order of Time Mages, you are found guilty of using forbidden magic, and of betraying your brothers and your order. You are found guilty of conspiring against our Lord, and of plotting to destroy what he has created. You have allied yourself with the enemy, and your sentence is death. Surrender now and it shall be swift and painless; do not, and you will suffer!"

A madman's laughter echoed across the battlefield, before Miller spoke: "You know nothing! I have found true power, the likes of which your precious Time Lord never could hope to control. I am a living god! Bow before my might, you pathetic worms!"

Miller raised his staff, and the Orcs rushed forth, stumbling toward the ranks of the combined army of Elves and men.

Moments later, the two frontlines crashed into each other. As the Orcs and soldiers of Efors stormed the allied ranks, several of the Corrupted Elves seemed to just disappear; others began firing arrows down onto the field.

From both sides, bolts and arrows rained down, as the combined ranks tried to hold off the onslaught. Before schedule, the cavalry rode in from the flanks. Some were immediately thrown from their frightened animals, as the High Cavalry and High Guard ordered their fighting horses to keep moving, kicking and biting the enemy as they were trained to do.

Chaos ensued, as the battle intensified and balanced. Blood was spilt on both sides; the advantage shifted back and forth, as arrows and bolts rained death on both armies. The Druids were kept busy keeping the sneaky Corrupted Elves at bay, while Larus and Larue joined to battle Miller behind them.

In their duel, corrupt and non-corrupt time magic was being hurled all over. Screams of death – from Elves, horses and Humans alike – could be heard, along with the agonized wailing of the Corrupted Elves , Efors soldiers and Orcs. Losses piled up on the sides, the bodies crushed beneath the alternately advancing armies.

After a long time of fighting, no one appeared to be gaining the upper hand, even with time mages, Druids and Lightors priests raining magic upon the enemy, and healing on the allies.

However, shortly the Corrupted Elves had gradually lost almost all of their close-combat, dagger-wielding troops; now it seemed that they were starting to retreat, in their manner: sneaking away. Noticing, and encouraged by this, the combined army pushed harder, causing the clumsy Orcs to tumble and stumble; once down, they were easy prey. The hundred or so Efors soldiers who had managed to push into the middle were now isolated, and were finding hard work of the stubborn fighters of the High Guard, and the elite Elven soldiers, armed with their glaives; they were making little progress. Wike and Turun, Tiri and Jiri were pushing back at them hard, while the protective backline gave covering fire and charged forward, with their daggers, knives and short-swords in hand.

Miller could see his army being destroyed, and began to accept the only action available to him: he gave Larus and Larue a final smirk and a dark wave, then disappeared, leaving his army leaderless.

Word soon began to spread through the dark troops that their leader had abandoned them, and they slowly started to panic. It wasn't long before they were inevitably beaten down.

The battle was won, but victory had come at a price – one perhaps too high for it to have been worth fighting: four-hundred Humans lay dead, Arlerk among them. The regular army and the

Order of Torsfor suffered the highest toll, with a combined 350 losses, ninety of which were from the order; their dead including Angel. The High Guard lost fifty men of their own, alongside three-hundred wounded.

150 Elves were dead, mostly those who bore glaives, though there were numbers amongst those in the front charge, with their daggers, too. A hundred Elves lay wounded.

In the aftermath of battle, many men did not speak. Many watched Iris, tired and battle-worn, dragging a crying and apparently wounded Scarlet with her, forcing the child to execute wounded enemies, and despatch those allies who could not be saved, with the stab of mercy; other squires could be seen doing the same duty, with their own daggers.

A group of female Orcs were spotted, stumbling out of hiding in a sand cave, before it collapsed. As they fled in terror, no one chased them.

Of the three-hundred allied horses, two-hundred were dead or dying. The time mages and Druids lost none of their number, but the priests of Lightors were not so lucky: ten of their brothers and sisters lay dead or dying.

The battle felt like an eternity at its most intense yet, despite the losses, in reality lasted no more than a mere twenty minutes. The battlefield was a sea of blood; it flowed all over, turning the sand red. Medics rushed out alongside the priests, Druids and time mages, to each do their bit, healing and carrying the wounded.

It had been a bloody day; a day to reflect on the blood shed on the ground, and what was saved by its being spilt. Were such high losses worth it? Only time will tell. That day was one I look away from: too bloody for my eyes.

After a week recuperating with the Elves, the Humans returned to their city; they arrived home two weeks later. The bodies were preserved by time mages, so that they could be given a proper hero's burial. Both cities declared three weeks of mourning, and the day of the battle would be marked every year by two days of respect to the fallen, and as a reminder of the evil which lurks in the wings, waiting for its opportunity.

The Orcs disappeared in Svaplar. I saw them myself, lured away by a creature which I have never before seen. I have no idea what it was, but I did find out, years later, what it does.

For now, though, my dears, let's leave them to grow, and start another story...

Chapter Three

The Demar People

(those who live in the Demar Mountain)

I am back, my dears, with another story to tell and a new adventure to follow.

This tale takes place only one year after the last. Yet, it actually begins during the days the preparations were being made in our previous story. At the same time that the Humans and Elves were planning their war, a Grassiak-based mining company was planning something else.

Known as the biggest and best of the mining guilds, Mina was planning to head for Rroker, to prospect based on a rumour. A special crystal was reported to be found upon a mountain known as Demar, in the middle of this rough terrain. The crystal was said to bring forth the great gifts of the earth. So, in secret, the guild made their plan, gathered their supplies from shady dealers and made sure to avoid any dealings with the law. Then, once the Human army had set off to battle, they made their move.

So, having dug tunnels under the city, some of which led all the way to the edge of Rroker, six brave miners left on their expedition.

Their boss was Rikar, his underboss Rikor, both brothers and middle-aged gentlemen. In the party were Mirak and Tirik, two young and curious female miners and treasure hunters; the girls were twins, though one was dark-haired, the other grey. Sig was a young lad, serving an apprenticeship with Rikar; his best buddy, Helgi, was also present, working his own apprenticeship for Rikor; both boys were fourteen years of age. The group were shorter than average in stature, none taller than around five-foot-six, and none smaller than five-foot – ideal candidates for working the low and narrow mineshafts.

Unbeknown to the group of explorers, what was to unfold was a tale of danger.

Underneath the city of Grassiak, in their secretly-dug tunnel, they were making preparations, thirty days before the army was to leave for war.

It was almost pitch-black inside the tunnels, except for some twenty candles scattered around the place, and one log fire. Rikar and Rikor were supervising a team of more than sixty miners, which included Mirak and Tirik, who were so eager to dig, they were always way ahead of the rest. Sig and Helgi were scurrying back and forth through the tunnels, bringing supplies and tools when needed, and removing blunted and broken tools for repair and sharpening.

"So, brother, how long will this take?" Rikar asked.

Rikor replied: "With Mirak and Tirik as eager as always, perhaps a month, if we're lucky." He appeared irritated and frowned. "Why did we end up taking so long to prepare for this project? We've known about the crystal for a long time, but only started digging five months ago."

Rikar shrugged. "It took longer than I thought it would to acquire all the gear we need for this."

Rikor sneered: "Well, leave the planning to me next time, brother."

"Yeah, yeah, brother," Rikar murmured, dismissively. He was already turning his attention to the workers; "Another ten metres of tunnel before we take a break, people. Get those pickaxes and shovels moving!"

Mirak shouted back: "Ten metres coming up, boss! Umm... I mean *bosses*."

Tirik was less enthusiastic; "Yeah, yeah. We can't work any faster than we already are. Ah! Something shiny!" She suddenly came running over, with a sizeable golden nugget in her hand, which she tossed into the bucket, itself engraved with a gold-leaf trim. Then, she hurried back into the tunnel, and dug on. The rest of the group glared at her, then shook their head at her glee, before they turned back to their work.

Slowly, bit by bit, the tunnel begun to take its shape. Only 170cm from floor to ceiling, it was wide enough for two normal-sized Humans to pass each other. The team worked in two thirty-person shifts: one through the night and one through the day – not that anyone could really ascertain the time.

In the morning, Rikor would say: "I'm going to sleep now, and get ready for the night shift. Be safe." Rikar would then nod, as Rikor made his way into a side tunnel, to sleep until the night came round again. Helgi would follow.

As the time passed, and five metres of tunnel had been dug, there would be a lunch break, usually around half-past-two in the afternoon; Rikor would signal Sig to go and check the time by returning to the base. Sig would then disappear for a while, with a candle, into the tunnel leading back to their base. Meanwhile, the rest would work on, themselves replacing any candles which burned out in the apprentice's absence.

On one occasion, when Sig was sent to check the time, they had reached almost two metres of finished tunnel before his return.

"What time is it roughly, Sig?" asked Rikar.

"It's dark outside, boss, so I would say shift change and evening meal."

"Right. Good boy. Break work, all! Wake the night shift and get something to eat, then get a good nap!"

People stopped their work, gratefully, and began wearily waking the sleeping night crew. They then cooked their meal on a fire in the tunnel, and ate before sleep.

This routine continued, on and on, day in and day out.

Thirty days later, the secret tunnel was complete.

People were lost in the dig. Most of the rear of the tunnel had collapsed behind them, killing men almost daily. By the time they were digging out the last remaining few feet, only thirty of the original sixty miners remained.

Mirak and Tirik crawled out first, onto the borders of Rroker, covered from head to toe in dirt and rock dust.

"Fresh air!" Mirak exclaimed.

"We have done it!" Tirik shrieked. "We are the best!"

Behind them, the others slowly came crawling out, carrying their backpacks. Tirik and Mirak helped them out. Before long, the rest of the team were breathing fresh air, for the first time in months.

After allowing them a well-deserved break, Rikor addressed the company: "We're moving out. Let's get this show on the road."

The group grabbed their backpacks and set to following Rikar; in his hand was a map of the mountainous region.

The harsh stone and rocky terrain soon tore away at the energy of them all; before long they decided to set up camp, rest up and wait for a new day. Tents were quickly set up, rocks dug or foraged, to anchor their guy-ropes to.

As day turned to night, they sat around the campsite, proudly reflecting on their achievement.

"We might have got this far," Helgi said, "but so many of us are gone."

Sig shrugged: "Whoever said that mining wasn't dangerous?"

Rikar interjected: "Sadly we lost people, yes, but that's how it sometimes goes with mining. But, we've survived, and we have to make sure this trip wasn't in vain."

Rikor was less emotive; "No time to mourn. We've got an objective to complete; there's no return from here now."

They spent the rest of the meal in silence, before hitting their sleeping sacks.

A new day rose, and the camp packed up. They set off immediately after breakfast.

It was a hard journey, with little to guide them, other than the mountains – but this was not enough to stop them. Day after day they travelled until, finally seeing their goal within reach, they picked up the pace. Demar was now only three to four days away, yet still they must pass deep gorges and narrow passes to reach it. The final leg was about to be undertaken.

As the crew of the Mina mining company set out on the dangerous part of their trek, they hoped that all of them would make it. The chapter would take half a day at least, its going slow, due to the steep and rocky terrain.

At one point they found themselves on a narrow ledge, ending in a deep gorge. Rikor took charge.

"Tie a rope around each other – lightest in the middle, heaviest up front, strongest and those of average weight at the back."

The team immediately started to do as the boss said, tying several ropes together and around each other's waistlines. Then, they tentatively started to move out, slowly making their way across their narrow edges; the drop was a long way down.

Suddenly finding themselves at a very sharp turn, one of the men in the middle of the chain slipped and fell, pulling the two on either side of him off of the rock-face. The rest of the team struggled and fought to pull them back up, desperately clinging not to fall themselves. But, they all knew that trying to pull up three was just too heavy; the man who fell first, and now hung suspended below, knew what he had to do, lest he put them all at risk. They all knew it, too.

"Good luck!" he called out, before cutting the rope-link around his waist; they watched him fall to his doom.

The two stragglers were pulled back to safety in an instant. All of the miners were in shock at the dreadful circumstances in which they had lost their colleague, but they were forced to move on, and Rikor quickly reached the other side.

The day passed too quickly, as they continued to teeter along the rock faces.   Finally, after what seemed like hours of balancing on narrow edges, they reached firm, safe ground.

And there it was, right in front of them: Demar.

Night would settle soon, so Rikor told them: "Untie yourselves and make camp. Let's get a fire going and make some food. We'll camp the night and start work tomorrow morning."

"Aye, boss," the miners said, in unison.

Quickly, a camp was built and a fire was made; rations of dried meat and fruit were cooked with water found in a creek in the rocks, nearby. They ate heartily, before heading into their tents for the night.

*

Early the next morning, people were up and about, doing their daily chores, while Rikar and Rikor were planning the work ahead.

Rikar proposed: "If we dig from here, we'll have a clear area to create a form of easy access; we can make a natural bottleneck."

Rikor was cautious. "We might, but how would we defend it, if need be? I say we wait a couple of years, until the Elves and Humans are trading, before we make our presence here transparent."

Rikar considered this and nodded. "I agree."

"Right, all gather round, people," Rikor called out.

As the company gathered before them, Rikar began to allocate tasks. "Sig and Helgi, make sure people get what they need; Tirik and Mirak, start digging a deep, wide entrance over there, and make it quick. The rest of you, get into your gangs and manage how you will support the girls, to dig deeper into the mountain; remember, this is unknown territory, people. Let's get started."

People immediately got to work. As Sig and Helgi got the tools ready for the men, Tirik and Mirak were already underway, digging into the side of the mountain, like termites on caffeine. Whilst awaiting specific plans, the rest of the team helped move the rocks to the side.

As the days passed, a wide entrance grew, and a tunnel drew deeper and deeper into the mountain. It was hard work, and required a great deal of expertise, such as digging granite by hand – a true skill, which very few possess. During late afternoons, hunting parties were sent out to get supplies.

As they dug, the tools became slower and more blunted, by the natural element of what would later come to be known as Demar steel – a rock as hard as granite, and as solid as steel. They were forced to heat the mountain with bellows and a furnace, and created a fortified alloy from it, with which to forge new tools.

Two weeks after it was created, Rikor and Rikar were greeted in the small area set aside for the furnace and homemade forge, by the blacksmith, Jarkres.

"Bosses, it is a pleasure to see you here."

Rikor and Rikar returned the greeting, then Rikar asked him: "Jarkres, how is the new ore?"

"As hard as granite and as solid as steel," Jarkres confirmed. "I think the new tools will last longer than anything we will encounter on this mountain."

Rikor grinned. "Well, I'll be damned; we might get rich from this in time."

Rikar agreed: "Indeed – in *time*. For now, let's just focus on digging."

Jarkres, still swollen with pride, continued: "I've named it Demar steel – it is completely novel. Please, give these to Tirik and Mirak." He handed them two finishing picks, forged of solid Demar steel.

Rikar took them, happily. "I will do that, while Rikor can get back to making sure all else is in order."

And, with that, Rikor and Rikar headed for the large entrance gates to Demar mines.

As Rikor went to check on the workers, Rikar made his way over to Tirik and Mirak, busy polishing the new gates, and handed them the picks. "Tirik, Mirak, try these new pickaxes."

Jumping down from their stone ladder, Tirik and Mirak took the pickaxes, immediately running excitedly into the barely-lit tunnel. Moments later, the sound of picks rapidly chipping away at rocks being could be heard.

"I guess they work," Rikar muttered to himself, before walking off to join his brother, and leave the girls to their work.

It would take another two years, and another five deaths, before they would even finish the grand tunnel, before starting work on a chamber inside.

However, very near the start of their adventure, they found something very worthwhile – now known as Demar Kingstone. It was something I found in another world, far away and long gone, and I will be truthful in that even I do not know its full power.

But, back to the tale of the Demar people...

One day, Tirik and Mirak came running out of the mines, excitedly, to the gates of the Demar mines. Tirik held a shining, clear-grey stone.

"Boss, look!"

"See what we got for you!" Mirak added.

Rikar and Rikor walked over to them, curiously taking the stone. With a hand each on it, they peered into its depths.

"Well, this is pretty," Rikar remarked. "Thanks, you two."

Rikor said: "It looks like something new. If we find more, I guess we'll see what it's worth." But, before he had even finished talking, Tirik and Mirak were already gone, scurrying back into the mine.

The small chamber was completed not long after the stone was found. In fact, over the span of the following year, they achieved greater productivity than ever before. You see, the stone was giving them power over the ground, and the rocks – I knew this to be the case, though I never how or why. As my time mages ensured peace in the land, I watched over the Demar people personally.

As they finished the chamber of the Demar mines, they called the miners to gather there. All came to hear what Rikor had to say.

"It is with great sadness that I must inform you all that Rikor has passed away, not long ago. I don't know how, nor why, but can only say that I am sorry he is now gone. I will assume full leadership. Meanwhile, I wish to show you all something."

The men were holding back silent tears, as they watched Rikar with growing curiosity.

In his hand, he held that shiny stone. Apparently no more than an ordinary stone with an extraordinary appearance, yet as he held it out toward a nearby rock, the rock started to reform before their eyes. Slowly, gradually, it began to shape into a statue, prettier than any hand-carved which any of the men had ever seen.

The tears began to subside, and the mood lightened at this amazing spectacle.

Rikar continued: "I found this stone by my bedside. I believe it to be something to do with that discovered by the girls a year or so ago. The previous night, I had a strange dream, in which I was speaking these words: *'By the people who live in Demar, I, as king, shall bestow the great power of earth and rocks to the people of Demar.'* "

Suddenly, as Rikar finished speaking those words, a grey beam of light emerged from the stone, projecting into every person in the chamber. Quite a panic ensued, but the ever-curious Tirik and Mirak simply looked downward, at the sudden appearance of two identical stones in the formation at their feet; they watched the glow of the small, shining rocks within the stones, those which formed their very pattern.

Simultaneously, they picked up their stones, touching them to the nearest rock; they watched in amazement, as the rock became a statue, just by their thinking it. They immediately called for the attention of the crowd, to show their discovery, and the panic ever so slowly died down.

And, suddenly, people were themselves carrying shining stones, appearing all around them, embedded in normal rocks.

"Look at what we can do, just by thinking it!" Tirik said, in awe.

"We've got boss power!" Mirak laughed.

All around them, people were trying their stones. To their amazement, they were creating their own statues – anything they could imagine.

"This is amazing," Rikar said. "Perhaps the dream was real."

Before long, Rikar made another announcement: "I propose that we form the Kingdom of Demar, ruled by us, the Demar people, and that we begin to test the limit of this magic – if that is what it is."

A shout of "Aye, boss!" went up around the place.

And, so the work commenced again.

With it began the story of the Kingdom of Demar and its people.

Rikar died four years later, in a mining accident. The rest I watch with a curious gaze. Over many years, they have changed, as have their descendants. Physically, they have evolved to live in the mines, growing to an average height of less than four feet tall.

Shortly later, another matter came to my attention: something was living in the swamps – not Human, Elven nor even Orc. I quickly sent a time mage, known as Silor, to investigate what it was. Do you wish to know what he discovered? Then, onward to the next story, my dear readers.

Chapter Four

The Svambar People

(half-Orc; half-Human)

Silor's report from the swamps was hasty in its arrival:

> *"I write this, as I send my thoughts and word to my Lord, the master of time. In this account I shall tell what I have witnessed on my inspection.*
>
> *"I arrived two days after receiving my Lord's message, in Svaplar. What I saw was amazing, yet frightening, too: creatures as tall as an Orc or a Human, yet which moved bent at the legs, almost hopping across the ground. And, another creature, far behind them, stood staring at me – the size of a dog, with skin like that of a snake; it disappeared shortly after. Before its departure, however, those people looked at me and said something which I did not understand; all were looking at me strangely. I decided to gift them the langue of time, in order that we may better understand each other. I would come to ask them something.*
>
> *"But, first, there were the events upon my arrival..."*

Svaplar, at the border.

Silor stood in the middle of their camp, surrounded by these half-creatures, speaking my word – the word of his Lord and the master of time.

"Lord of Time, grant me the honour of bestowing upon these people your word, your learnings and your speech. Let them talk, like all do in the land; let them become one of your chosen. I beg this of you, so that I may, as your servant, learn who they are."

And, so it was that I gave them my gift. I did so to learn more, but also because I had a firm hunch that these were the descendants of the Orcs who had gone missing here – although, I had no knowledge to confirm this. But, let us get back to the story...

A blue-white light washed over the creatures, as Silos spoke in a clear and friendly voice: "Who in this camp will speak with me about your people?"

One of the creatures immediately hopped forward, with a wooden staff in his hand. "I, Aklar, shall speak for my people, as the Lord of Svamp and their spiritual guide."

Another stepped forward. "I am Makarak, the leader of our people; I shall listen, strange one."

Silor followed the two into a shabby-looking tent, and sat on the ground before them. "Tell me, who are you people?" he asked. "How did you come here, and how are you familiar to my Lord and master of time?"

Aklar leaned forward. "I will tell you our tale. We are Svambar people, as translated by your tongue. We came into existence no more than two years ago; we are an offspring of Measeri, the god of the swamps, born of Orc and Human. We possess both of their strengths, but also many of our own weaknesses; as you can see, we cannot run or walk as normal, but rather crouch and jump and skip – yet we can stand upright."

Silor listened with interest, meditating the words to his Lord, before speaking once again. "I understand. I was informed that my Lord suspected your relation to the missing Orcs, but not how. I shall relay all that we discuss to my fellow mages, and see if we can help you to become a better, more prosperous people.

"Now, let me ask, how do your ranking and status structures work?"

Makarak was about to speak, but a raised hand from Aklar quickly silenced him.

"Makarak is our leader – our 'kingska', or *king* in your tongue," Aklar explained. "Then, we have the bladir, the kingska's personal guards, and our elite warriors. Beneath them we have the regular arkska – our army – and its leader, Arkbak. Then, there are the common folk. We allow slaves, however, we permit this role to only be assigned to those which are willing to undertake it – I personally control the enforcement of this."

Silor once again meditated the words to his Lord, the master of time, before speaking: "Myself and my fellow mages will arrange a meeting between you and the other peoples of this land, on neutral ground. Please understand now though that there is a great hatred for Orcs – hence the need for neutral ground."

"Very well," Aklar agreed, "we shall see what happens. Emeary thuse maste gauer; may the swamps open a path of guidance."

All rose and bowed as Silor left the tent, before teleporting back to the tower.

Silor arrived very quickly at the Time Tower in Icres, and immediately sent word to Larus and Larue, as well as another mage, named Iksas.

They gathered in a circle, in a large room on the middle floor of the Time Tower, readying for Silor to speak.

"My fellow mages, I gather you for the matter of the rumours in Svaplar. I have seen a new people there, and have given them our Lord's gift. The issue lies in the fact that they are half-Orc and half-Human, which is why I wish to gather the Humans and Elves for a meeting. After introductions have been made between them, I wish the Demar people to be made aware of them also – that I will leave in the hands of Iksas."

Iksas nodded. "Very well. That I shall do, once we are done here."

"I shall relate this to the Humans," said Larus. "I am sure I can persuade their wise new king and queen of the benefits."

Larue concurred: "I shall do the same. It will be more difficult, as the Elves hold a great hatred toward the Orcs. Still, I will do my very best to talk it through with them."

"That is all I can ask of you, my brothers," said Silor. "Time be with us all."

With that, all bowed before taking their leave, each to depart to their respective locations.

Iksas arrived at the gate to the Demar mine. Only a handful of local guards were standing watch, their magic quickly locking the gate. One of the guards bellowed: "Halt! Who goes there and what is your purpose?"

Iksas removed his hood, calling back to them: "I am Iksas, of the time mages. I wish to speak to your king, in the name of the Lord of Time and his servants."

"You may pass, but be respectful, and do not stray from the main road." The guards reopened the gates, and Iksas walked forward, bowing to them as he passed through.

He followed a barely-lit road, farther into the mine. Before long, he came upon a great doorway, with at least four guards standing before it – it was quickly sealed, as they signalled for him to halt. Rakta, a guard of the inner gate, demanded: "You there, stop and tell me your business here, or you will be buried in this very stone."

Iksas remained calm. "I come on behalf of the time mages and the Lord of Time. I wish to speak to your king, regarding matters of alliance and trade."

"Very well," Rakta replied. "Wait here while I relay your message to the king; he will decide if you are worthy of entering our halls." With that, Rakta opened the door and disappeared inside.

An age seemed to pass before he re-emerged. "You may speak to the king. Bow before you speak and keep your tone respectful."

Iksas nodded and followed Rakta into the Demar mine's throne hall. Inside, Iksas followed.

They were shortly approaching an unusually tall Demar man, sitting on a stone throne; he held a crystal in his hand. Rakta stopped a few metres in front of him, then turned to face down Iksas.

Iksas bowed toward the Demar on the throne: King Romboka.

"You may speak to me," the king told him, "but be aware that one wrong move and you will die."

"Your honoured kingship, I am Iksas, of the time mages; I come on behalf of the time mages and the Lord of Time. In a few days' time, there will be a meeting between a new race of people, the Humans and the Elves. My fellow mages and our Lord wish to ask you to meet with them afterward, to discuss trade and a possible alliance between your people and theirs. This is to ensure that all races can stand together, and ensure their survival and defence, should a common enemy emerge. Furthermore, economy shall flourish with cooperation; we do not grow by insular socialization, and we gain no new knowledge. This we humbly ask of you, your kingship."

Romboka considered the pitch. "It sounds like a very solid request. However, I will need to present this to the Demar council, as a matter which regards all of our people. Rakta, go and gather them now, for an emergency meeting. Iksas, if you will wait outside the door, Rakta will return to inform you of what is decided by the council."

"I shall await your decision, your kingship." Iksas bowed as he left unattended, Rakta having already disappeared to carry out his orders.

Sitting patiently outside the Demar mine's throne hall, Iksas could hear a lot of yelling and bickering, through the heavy stone door. Iksas tried to block out the dissenters, meditating as he waited.

After what felt like hours, Rakta finally came out of the throne room, to deliver the council's message: "It has been decided that the council will personally attend the meeting with the new people, and will consider what they deem to be the benefits of alliance. They do not promise anything, but are open to talks."

Iksas bowed. "That is all we ask. I shall await you at this location." Iksas handed Rakta a map, before bowing once again and taking his leave. Rakta took the parchment, returning the bow, before returning through the stone doors.

*

Larue arrived at the home of the King of Elves, teleporting in front of his majestic tree. He knocked on the wooden door before entering.

As he entered, Tiri and Jiri stood and bowed slightly; Larue returned the gesture with a bow of his own.

Tiri smiled. "You don't look a day older, felan. Please, what brings you here?"

Larue said, warmly: "Greetings, Elven king and prince. I have come to arrange another meeting, with a certain race of people, recently discovered. Let me tell the tale."

Larue proceeded to explain the story of the Svambar people to them. Afterward, Tiri nodded, thoughtfully. He was just about to speak, when Jiri whispered something into his ear. When Jiri was done speaking, Tiri said: "My dear son advocates that we go and meet them; we give them a chance. I grow older as the days go by, and I listen more readily to my successor, so that he may rule something he should be proud of, like my father and grandfather before me.

"We shall depart shortly. We shall meet you at the time-hut, I presume?"

Larue smiled. "At the hut, indeed. Farewell, King of Elves."

Tiri bowed. "Farewell, my felan. May we meet again under pleasant terms." They bowed to one another again, before Larue teleported away.

At the Human capital, Larus arrived at the entrance to the King's hall. The guards allowed him passage without question.

Inside, he quickly marched toward the throne room, where the high guards let him pass into the room. Larus entered and knelt immediately before the royal couple.

The current king, Amarks, was seated beside the leader of the Humans, Queen Scarlet, now a fully-grown and well-built young woman. Her voice betrayed a touch of surprise at his presence; "Larus, what brings you here, old man?"

Larus replied: "I came to deliver a message – and a story – youngling."

Larus commenced telling the same story as Larue. When finished, he looked at the couple for their response.

Scarlet was pensive. "I see that my father and mother were not wrong to allow the retreating Orcs their freedom, all those years ago. I will attend the meeting... if my dear husband agrees?"

"Of course, my beloved," Amarks confirmed. "I never waiver from your side – you know that."

Larus smiled. "Excellent! Meet us at the same hut that your father and mother attended all those years ago, for their talks with the Elves."

"Very well," Scarlet agreed. "I shall gather my guards and a small force, and we shall head out shortly."

Larus nodded as he left the throne room, without speaking another word. Amarks and Scarlet looked curiously at him as he left, before Amarks enquired: "What's with him?"

Scarlet chuckled. "He just a touch old, and a tad weird; nothing to worry about."

Amarks slowly nodded, deciding to leave it at that.

A few days later, they met inside the time hut.

Scarlet and Amarks were on one side of the table, accompanied by a young woman and another. Beside them were Tiri and Jiri, along with the ever-lovely Druid leader, Silir, standing, thankfully, in a robe.

On the other side of the table were Aklak and Makarak, of the Svambar people. A small party of Svambar were with them. Silor stood with Larus and Larue, at the end of it.

Silor spoke first: "We are gathered today to discuss alliance and trade, between a group of people amongst whom there is a shared mix of love and hatred. The Svambar people wish to consign the behaviour of their ancestors to the past, and promise to do better by them in the future. However, they do have certain conditions for such – thus, we hold this meeting.

"The Demar mine people shall join the talks later, to discuss trade and possible shared defences – and, perhaps more potential alliances. Are we all clear that this is neutral ground, and that no hostile actions shall ever be undertaken here – in the name of our time lord?"

All parties raised their hands in agreement.

Satisfied, Silor once again spoke: "Let us begin with introductions; our names and ranks. The Svambar people may open."

Aklak was the first to speak up: "I am Aklak, elder, shaman

and speaker of the Lord of the Svamp; to put it simply, I am a spiritual guide for our people."

Makarak was next, standing tall and proud. "I am Makarak, kingska – or king – of the Svambar people. I lead all."

A young female appeared from the shadows behind her kingska, and spoke up in broken language: "I Blasaderi Imeri, of Svambar people – leader the bladir, elite warriors of our people."

Another woman, middle aged, appeared beside her; "I Saklak Akbar. Lead army warriors."

Silor gestured toward the Elves. Tiri nodded and said: "I am Tiri, King of Elves."

Jiri was next, aiming a curious gaze toward the new people. "I am Jiri, prince of the Elves and successor to the throne."

Silir spoke next, her gaze a furtive and distrusting one. "I am Silir, leader of the Druids, the spiritual guides of our people."

Silor nodded his acknowledgement to the Elves, then turned to the Humans.

Scarlet was the first to speak, her tone a confident one. "I am Queen Scarlet, leader of the Humans and descendant of the first king and queen of the Humans."

Amarks spoke next, firm yet soft: "I am King Amarks, the second leader of the Humans and husband to our dear queen."

The young woman of the two people accompanying the Humans stood up, speaking with an almost divine tone; "I am Angel Imira, spiritual leader of the Humans, blessed by Lightors himself." Imira sat down again.

The ageing man alongside her stepped forward, speaking with a rusted tongue: "I am Isak, commandor of the amyr."

Just as Isak stepped back, a tall, middle-aged woman entered the hut, in full High Guard uniform and armour. "Do excuse my lateness, my queen and honoured guests; I had a few disciplinary issues in need of being dealt with. Please forgive my manners: I am Irilie, high captain of the High Guard." Irilie bowed, as she went to take her position beside Scarlet.

Unnoticed, another older man had entered the room behind her, and he now spoke up. "Excuse me; I am growing old and slow. I am Tira of the Negpol; I am here to help smoothly facilitate political matters."

Silor nodded to acknowledge conclusion of the introductions. Then, without delay, he gestured toward the swamp people to put forth their demand.

Aklak spoke up, decisively: "We wish to ally and trade with your peoples, but we are aware of your views of slavery. Nevertheless, we require allowance to keep our culture of voluntary slavery; it is important to acknowledge that they willingly consent to their enslavement, and their reasons for so doing. To ensure this stipulation is met, I propose to put in place a specialized enforcement team, which will assess each contract and application for a registered slave which comes in. I am prepared to personally lead this team, though I would like it to include a representative of each race, selected by the leaders of their people."

Scarlet stood up to address the proposal; "I see no issues with this matter. Illegal slavery exists, there is no denying that fact – our friend's proposal could in fact help to reduce illegal slavery, putting in place firm guidelines for its enforcement."

Tiri was already nodding his agreement, as Jiri spoke up: "I would agree with that statement, Queen Scarlet. As a matter of fact, we have been dealing with many attempts of kidnapping and trafficking, including successful ones on our people. As it appears that the Humans are also aware of this problem, the opportunity to see something firmly being done to control it is its own reason. As the future king of my people, I wish to make it known that I want to ally with the swamp people."

Tiri nodded his agreement, happy and proud to allow his son to take the lead on this decision; he could already see that his son bore the qualities needed to lead their people.

Silor addressed the table again: "I can assume then that we all agree to the terms? If so, please raise your hand." All hands went up in agreement, without hesitation.

Iksas entered just as they were wrapping up, and nodded toward Silor, who immediately, once again, spoke up.

"As you know, many years ago, some Humans relocated to the Demar mountains to mine, where they formed a new people. I have invited their representatives here to discuss trade and a defensive alliance."

At this, six of the mining people entered, still dressed in their filthy work clothes, and stood at the far end of the table. Two of the group clearly resembled aged versions of Tirik and Mirak. The Demars stood on stone chairs to speak, so that they could be clearly seen.

Silor indicated for them to speak, though only Romboka addressed the table. "The council of the Demar people has agreed that I, Stone King Romboka, shall speak for us. Tell me, which of you will speak for your peoples."

Jiri raised his hand. "I will speak for the Elves, as permitted by my father." Tiri nodded his consent.

Tira spoke next: "I, Tira, shall speak on behalf of my queen and king."

"I, Shaman Aklak, shall speak for the Svambar people."

Silor proceeded to speak again: "I have asked the Demar people to put forth their own demands, which we shall consider."

Romboka instantly said: "I demand fair trade, and a concession that we shall only present our miners in defence of an existential or life-threat; we are miners, not soldiers. In return, we shall build a trade road to our gates and a market square in front."

Tira considered for a moment, before concluding: "These are fair terms indeed. But, how are we to uphold them? And, what do you have to offer us, in respect of traded goods?"

Jiri interjected: "Might I also merely question what defensive abilities you have to offer, as miners?"

Aklak simply said: "As long we are allowed to keep our volunteer slaves, across any races, we are happy."

Romboka looked at each of them in turn, before answering: "My miners have the power of the Demar Mountain; we can shape earth and rocks at will – we have only to ask. My Kingstone gives us the power to do so. We offer the finest and hardest ores that exist; we can forge weapons, tools and armour however they should be needed, and we can craft anything from the elements of the earth with little more effort than a thought. We will even trade our knowledge of how to achieve this – for a price, of course.

"The same goes for the volunteer slaves: we are happy to concur, as long as we get a say in its implementation. Furthermore, we propose, among each race the appointment of a trade master, who shall take a quarter of all goods sold, and split the profits evenly between all the races."

Tira whispered an exchange with his queen and king, before speaking again. "We concur to these demands, and we deem them fair. We shall appoint a royal trader to overlook this taxation, and we will form a new order of 'Makairs' – an order of traders and craftsmen – to carry out the work."

Jiri nodded; "The Elven agree to this, and pledge to uphold a fair-trade treaty."

Aklak proposed an amendment: "Each race's representative must be required to swear an oath that their slave will not be required to carry out orders which may bring dishonour to their own race."

All looked at Aklak, then all nodded their approval.

Silor looked them over once more, to see if anyone had anything else to add, before saying: "If each of you have nothing more to say, I propose to call an end to this meeting, and to let us depart in peace.

"Time, guide us all, in the name of the Lord of Time."

All around the table began to chatter and discuss in a more relaxed tone, particularly the religious members and the leaders. Another hour or so passed, before they even started to depart the time hut and begin their long journeys home.

And so, here we are, having explained all of our backgrounds, and accounted for how I made this land and the people shaped it.

Ten years after this meeting, I have a story to impart, having managed to procure a copy, written from the viewpoint of a young Elven slave, who goes by the name Liremir. I will let her start it off, pitching in for context of the bigger picture.

Any subsequent story is for another time and place, so may time preserve you all until then.

Chapter Five
The First Combined Army

I am back, my dears, with another exciting story to tell, as told to me by my time mages.

Ten long years passed before all the recommendations of the historic trade meeting were implemented and operational; the Humans' Order for Trade and Craft alone took five years to really get up and running. Now, trade is flowing as freely as the rivers.

The introduction of the Slave Law took ten years, after its rules, clauses and amendments bounced back and forth (about which I shall explain more, when I am done relating these stories). Let's see what this young Elven slave tells, of how it all begun.

The recorded account by Liremir:

"Greetings. I am Liremir, slave to my beloved master, the ingska, now kingska of the Svamp people – or, as he was when I came to meet him, prince of the Svamps. I have been asked by the time mage Silor, to provide a first-person's glimpse at what transpired on that fateful day, almost twenty years ago.

"I recall it as a calm morning. I was called into the hyr house, to talk of my request to be enslaved among the Svamp people – even though I am Elven. You see, it is little-known among outsiders, but I am an adopted daughter of the vingara. My family were killed in the two wars: the one prior to this, and the one here now. The vingara was kind enough to take me as his own, even though he has not yet found a soulmate.

"Let me see if I can present the time mage a first-person view of my

memories, that they may one day be relayed to some unknown reader..."

In the Golden Forest, a young, slender, yet densely muscled Elven woman entered the hyr house, bowing to Jiri and Tiri, stood in counsel by the window, at the far end of the first room. "You called, my hyr, Vingara?"

Tiri looked at her with a sigh, while Jiri simply addressed her calmly: "I have told you, you are to call us by our names, or by the family name, Liremir. But, forget that; I am told you wish to enter the slave system, under the recent legislation. You are aware that this can cost you your life, and that you will be little more than a mere object of your master's will – as long as it does not dishonour your race, of course?" He added this last comment a little sardonically.

Liremir nodded. "I am aware of this, Vingara, but it is what I want. I am tired of being in this place; I need to go exploring, to find my own way, but you know I also prefer others to be in control. This seems like the ideal way of achieving my goals, but under a firm hand."

Tiri and Jiri both looked at her and nodded, with a sigh. Tiri told her: "We know this. That is why I spoke with your adopted father: we agreed to let you go, but you are always free to come home again, whenever you wish, my grand-daughter."

Liremir nodded. "I understand. I know it is a mutual agreement, between master and slave. If that is no longer the case, the contract and oath are broken."

Jiri agreed: "Indeed so. Be careful, young one; I would hate to see you get hurt, or worse."

Liremir hugged them both, warmly. "Thank you for all you have done. It is now time to find my own path – a path which I want to follow."

She left to pack her belongings, in a room not far from theirs. Not long after, she emerged dressed in her armour, with a bow on her back, and a quiver hanging on each side of her body; a knife was tucked into the back of the belt, below her backpack. She waved goodbye to her empty home, as she walked out of the door.

Outside, Liremir ran toward a nearby tree, walking the last few metres, to knock on the door. A middle-aged Elven man peeked out.

"Excuse me," Liremir asked, "would you happen to be representative for Elves who wish to enslave themselves?"

The Elven man replied: "That be me; Eracuse. Have you got the hyr and vingara's permission? I am well aware that you have been adopted by the vingara. If the answer is yes, then please come in."

Liremir nodded: "I have. Let's get this done, shall we?"

At that, he opened the door for her to pass, and they both stepped inside. Eracuse made his way over to a fine, wooden chair, magically carved from the very tree itself. He sat and indicated for Liremir to sit opposite, on a simple stool in front of him; Liremir sat without argument.

Eracuse handed over some paperwork, before he started to speak. "I need your full name, lineage, next of kin, objectives and intentions, and... ahem... any unusual habits." The last words he hinted at meaning something illicit or suggestive.

Without hesitating, Liremir took the pen and ink nearby, writing carefully. Once finished, she put the papers down and waited for him to read it. Eracuse picked them up and looked through intently, before stamping them.

He turned back to her. "Now, if you would be so kind as to sign here, we will move downstairs for a physical examination."

Liremir signed the sheet, before following Eracuse down his

spiral staircase.

Liremir wrote:

> "I shall spare you the details of what happened, but let's just say that he knows all of me by now. Anyway, following that, I was placed into a cage. I waited for a day or so, before myself and others were put and locked into a cage-cart, bound for the newly built city of Svamgar, home to the Svamp people.
>
> "It took us a whole month to reach the place. First sight of it was amazing: a single-level city, with walls of wooden palisades and mud, surrounded on all sides by swampland. In the middle of the city was a hill, with a small mud enclosure and a grand hall – all in the same colours as the swamp.
>
> "The cart was held near the gate, as some Svambar warriors came to check. Eracuse already had all the papers ready, and it didn't take us long to enter the city itself. Inside, it was very crowded. We were taken toward a large building. As the cart stopped in front of it, Eracuse jumped out and unlocked our cage. Four Svambar warriors took us inside, while Eracuse had our personal gear taken away, into a room next to the staircase we were about to descend.
>
> "We were held in the basement, as we nervously awaited a master. It wasn't long before someone came in and yelled out for all the female Elves present to stand up, and to follow, in no more than the rags we were given. This, we did."

They were taken to the Slave Presentation Hall. The four Elven females were brought in and roughly pushed into a line, to wait.

Shortly, Aklak entered the room and yelled out: "The ingska, our prince, wishes to buy a slave. He has insisted – against his father's wishes – upon an Elf. Please, stand still while he inspects you."

A tall, young Svambar man entered, in full bladir armour, with four fellow bladirs around him. With the looks of a tall, wide and muscular Human male about his upper body, he had a strong Orcish lower half. His head appeared more Human than Orcish, his green skin tinged with enough tone of the light-tanned Human. He glared at the slaves.

"I, Ingska Malla'ak, wishes slave Elven. Me look you."

Malla'ak walked forward, looking over each of the Elves, before stopping to examine Liremir more closely. After some deliberation, he decided: "Me like Elf her. Me want. Me take Elf."

Aklak nodded, signalling to the guards to take the rest downstairs, while Liremir was told to follow him and Malla'ak. They led Liremir into a room with a half-circle table and four chairs. Eracuse was already waiting for them there. He nodded to Aklak, who stepped over beside him.

Aklak then turned to address them, still in the doorway: "Will the slave and master please step in front of the table and swear the oath."

As she and the prince entered the room, Eracuse handed Liremir a note, nodding at her to begin reading it.

"I, slave Liremir, hereby swear my loyalty and dedication to my master. I shall do my utmost to complete my duties. I swear not to dishonour my master's race, and I understand that he is dutybound to the same."

Eracuse nodded his approval at her oration, before turning his attention toward Aklak, who tipped his own nod toward Malla'ak.

"I, Ingska Malla'ak, future kingska Svambar, swear take slave. Loyalty all to be broken; not dishonour race."

Aklak nodded again, prompting Eracuse to finish the ceremony. Eracuse rounded up: "Then, by the oath sworn, I declare that both of you are rightfully slave and master. Take good care of each other, respect each other, and you will have a better slave and master relationship. We shall keep your contract on record, and if any issues arise in the future, we are here to help."

All bowed then, as Malla'ak prepared to speak: "Slave follow. Bladir get slave equipment; slave guard me."

Liremir tipped her head; "Yes, Master; slave will follow you." She followed Malla'ak out of the room, closely followed by the Bladir.

"I followed my master about, as he cast inspection over the warriors and bladirs in training. We returned to the hall later that day.

"I was only given my knife, and remained in rags. I was not permitted to speak unless Master was threatened, so I didn't speak at all.

"I am slightly embarrassed at how I started my life as a slave; that first night was painful. I shall spare you the details, but suffice to say that, even with healing, I will never walk like a normal Elf again! Still, it is a small price to pay for a master of this status.

"Time went by, as it always did. I would usually follow Master around; if not, I would kneel at his feet, waiting, with a dagger nearby. I felt safe with him, even though I was mostly his personal guard dog, and I value that trust yet.

"There have been signs of unrest for a while, but what has happened now was never expected. It all started when word came that a group of rebels was besieging the Human capital; my master was ordered by the kingska to take half of the arkska and sixty bladirs with him to their aid. He would lead them, while the kingska would stay and maintain order here, with the remainder of the army. So it was that we set out.

"It took us almost two months to reach the Human capital of Grassiak. I was fully equipped and never once strayed a mere yard away from my master. On the way, we met up with half of the Dieferdar, also on their way to assist the Humans – they were led by none other than my adopted father. He addressed my master, saying that he hoped the future king of the Svambar was keeping his daughter safe. My master merely *replied that I will be, as long as I do my job. I remained silent throughout the exchange, and followed them as they talked casually, all the way to the Human capital."*

The Human capital of Grassiak was under siege.

Liremir arrived alongside Malla'ak and Jiri, with the bladir, arkska and Dieferdar behind them, to see the gates and walls under attack from a large army, at least a thousand strong.

Malla'ak didn't hesitate to give the order: "Arkska, bladir, charge! Honour, blood us!"

With that, the thousand-strong Svambar arkska charged proudly into battle, shouting and yelling in glory. The bladir were right behind Malla'ak, who charged in immediately after the arkska; Liremir did her best to keep up.

Jiri, however, was more cautious. "Dieferdar, stay at maximum range to give air cover." The Elves moved swiftly to position and drew their bows.

Already, from the other end of the field, the yells of death could be heard. While the Humans were managing to hold off the attack, half of the besieging army retreated, to turn and switch its focus to its own rear, as the arkska went crashing into the enemy, in a din of metallic chaos. Most were clad in chainmail, or brigandine armour, with gambeson underneath; it was a brutal melee, with weaponry of all kinds. The arkska themselves were barely clad, in chainmail or boiled, waxed leather armour.

Both sides took heavy losses very quickly. However, when Malla'ak and the bladirs crashed into the battle, the allies began to fare well, due to the plate armour they wore. Liremir kept close, doing her very best to defend Malla'ak.

Arrows rained down, courtesy of the Elves behind, and the

enemy reciprocated, with a good arsenal of spring-loaded bows. Losses were piling up on both sides, when the enemy were given the order to focus on defending. The moment they did so, of course, the gates to Grassiak opened, and the High Guard attacked. Scarlet and Amarks, with Irilie in front, led the charge at full gallop. Beside Irilie was mounted a young girl, apparently no older than fourteen years. Troops charged the enemy on horseback and on foot, as horns and drums sounded behind them. All the while, arrows and bolts from spring-loaded bows hailed down the city walls.

Now massively outnumbered, the enemy began to panic and flee. The fight was over very quickly after that.

Two hundred arkska lay dead, in contrast to only three of the bladir. The Elves suffered forty losses; with fortune, most of their casualties were injured and treated. Over seven-hundred of the enemy were killed, the field red with their blood.

Scarlet, Amarks, Irilie and the young girl approached where Malla'ak and Jiri gathered, Liremir standing dutifully to the side of them.

"I see my letters reached you," said Scarlet. "Thank you for coming to our aid. I am sad for your losses. That is how battle goes."

Malla'ak was more philosophical: "Queen Scarlet, losses not matter; dead honour death."

Jiri appeared a little more distressed, though he hid it admirably. "It was my pleasure to lend aid, Queen Scarlet, just as your people have aided mine in the past."

Nor could Jiri hide his concern; "These rebels appear not to have been working alone. Could this assault be related to the ambush your mother and father were subjected to?"

Scarlet looked worried by the prospect. "I pray that is not the case. We must find whoever is responsible."

Suddenly, Aklak came running, out of breath, and yelling: "Arsac City has fallen. The rebels attacked after you left, Ingska. Your father wishes for you to hurry back, gather any allies you can and retake the city for yourself. I was sent ahead by the kingska, to inform you."

Malla'ak appeared furious at the news, and proceeded to kick and beat poor old Aklak so hard that he could barely stand. "Bah, idiot!" he cursed. "You are no longer Head Shaman; I shall find one worthier of the post. Coward be gone!"

Aklak stumbled away, fearful of the future kingska's mood. As everyone else, Liremir watched the scene in silence, without comment.

Scarlet simply shook her head at Malla'ak's display. Still, she pledged: "Give us five days, and we will gather a good-sized company to assist in retaking your city. We will also send word to the Demar people, to come to your aid. This is a matter of trade: it will dissolve if the rebels keep power."

Jiri added: "I will send word to my father. We shall send the dead home and request reinforcements to meet at the Crossroads, in five days' time."

Malla'ak nodded his approval, explaining: "Shaman coward; allies not cowards. Me army camp wait; take city ours." At this, the bladir arkska cheered their now acting-king, for being strong and showing leadership.

As Liremir started to prepare her master's tent, her hands began to shake with fear.

The camp didn't take long to set up, consisting mostly of poles covered with hides. Basic sleeping skins serviced most of those present, except for the ingska, whose bed was assembled. Liremir would be left to sleep on the ground, or in his bed – whichever took his fancy.

The bodies of the dead were stacked in a mass grave and

burned.

Liremir would write:

> "We camped there for five days, before a company of some two-thousand humans came along, led by two women, the queen and king having left the commandor in charge for now. One of the women was Irilie; the other was apparently Princess Turuk. Both looked fearsome, much as their queen and king, though Turuk appeared anxious also.
>
> "My adopted father sent the dead home, and revived another hundred Elves to aid him, with word that the hyr would join later, accompanied by several Druids (this number would not include Silir, who was tasked with guarding our home).
>
> "We left early in the morning, the dead on my master's side having been burned the day after the battle. Now, even more will die – I pray I will not be among them. Yet, I follow my master until he dies – or until I do. I love him, despite his fits of rage, which he has a tendency to display over the smallest thing. Still, he is a good person."

My dears, I will continue to tell you the story of Liremir, to afford you the best viewpoint of the battle yet to come, and how the tale will unfold. It is an exciting one, I assure you, but a frightening one also, with many twists along the way. Let us return to it...

The Crossroads, in Rroker, intersected roads leading to the Humans, Elves, Demar and Svambar people.

After two months travelling, the combined army of the Svambar, the Elves and the Humans arrived there. Two lively, middle-aged women awaited them, with a party of twenty.

"Hello there," Tirik greeted them. "The Stone King sends his regards."

Mirak added: "He has sent us to help you, as it concerns him that trade will fail if the rebels take power; we have already recorded less trade since this uprising began."

"So, here we are, ready to give you a hand – as best we are able. I am Tirik, by the way."

"And, I am Mirak. Both of us are on the council for the Demar people."

Malla'ak was the first to respond: "I Malla'ak, ingska of Svambar."

Jiri nodded to the women, calmly. "You already know me."

Scarlet spoke in more of a rush: "And us, of course. The young one there is our dear daughter, Turuk." Scarlet pointed to the child.

Clearly not wishing to spend any more time on introductions, Malla'ak signalled it was time to move on.

The combined army went with haste, knowing that the sooner they arrived, the sooner battle could commence.

It took them another month to reach the Svambar capital of Arsac. The city was already on high alert, as the combined army camped on a dry clearing of land, a safe distance away.

A large, tactical tent was quickly raised by the Humans, in which to plan operations. The moment it was ready, each of the leaders made their way inside, Turuk following her mother's footsteps. Scarlet, Turuk, Amarks, Malla'ak, Mirak, Tirik and Jiri gathered around a table in the centre, which was covered by a large map.

"These are the only plans we have of the city," said Scarlet, "and then only because we helped design it. I'm sure the ingska can give us more accurate information."

Malla'ak looked at them all, then at Liremir. "Slave know.

Slave talk."

Liremir looked surprised, yet dared not question or say otherwise. "Yes, Master. If I may have something with which to draw, I shall explain."

Jiri tossed her a piece of charcoal, which Liremir caught, and started to draw on the map as she explained: "First of all, we have a big market and craft fayre, just inside the gate. It is usually crowded and heavily guarded. The right side leads to the poor alley, for those not worthy of anything; on the left is the barracks and training ground for the arkska – so, if you can cut that off, it would help. As you move forward, toward the hall, to the left side the leadership and the elite five warriors of both the arkska and bladir are housed. Here are also the bladir barracks and training pit, as well as a dungeon – apparently for training only; I recommend blocking this off—"

Before Liremir could proceed any further, Malla'ak smacked her across the face. "Dungeon make strong warriors. Best."

Liremir simply took the assault and nodded. "I'm sorry, Master." As if nothing had happened, she returned her attention to the group. "At the kingska halls, you will likely face the best which can be fielded, of the arkska and any bladir which can be assembled. Most of them will be posted near the king – or, should I say, their false king. My master is now the true kingska."

Jiri put his hand on his chin and thought for a few moments, before speaking. He understood Liremir's meaning. "Whoever this false king is, he must have some great fighters among his ranks, if he was able to overthrow the former kingska... who we must assume is now dead. This is not going to be an easy fight."

Malla'ak simply added, apathetically: "Father weak; me strong. Me lead better; me fight better."

They all looked at Malla'ak for a second, with their own

thoughts, before Tiri entered the tent, bowing to them. "Sorry I am late. I had to secure our homes; the Corrupted Elves have been increasingly harassing us."

Scarlet looked at him. "That is not good. I could make an outpost on the border, should you wish, to ensure that they don't dare attack."

Tiri looked at Jiri, who nodded: "We very much welcome aid; we can't be on guard all the time and still go about our business."

"That much is clear, indeed," replied Scarlet. "I will get word to the commandor, once we return."

Tiri got busy looking at the map. He pointed at something, before saying: "This smaller entrance, at the back, is for rituals and such – correct?"

Malla'ak confirmed: "Shaman passage. Secret. Emergency in case."

Everyone studied the map, then looked back at Tiri. Scarlet was the first to answer: "If you are thinking as I do, King Tiri, then I propose that we bombard the walls with range fire from here... if we are to send a small party around to carry out a surprise attack. When the guards are distracted by the small party, we can force the gates and storm in from here, taking the city without need to destroy it or kill any civilians."

Malla'ak nodded, as he offered: "Kill civilian not honour."

Jiri added: "There is no need to kill any civilians. Furthermore, it would be simply wrong."

All nodded their agreement to the plan. Liremir raised her hand, looking at Malla'ak for permission to speak; he merely nodded, as she stood. "If I may, I suggest that we send no more than six people from each race around to the back. We should keep the numbers low, yet sufficient to fight. I suggest we send only the strongest and most loyal." Liremir then lowered back down to her knees, careful not to get her master angry again.

With a touch of indifference, Malla'ak said: "Slave right. Slave good. Me take six bladirs."

Scarlet nodded her agreement, as she replied next: "I will send Turuk, with six high guards and Irilie for support."

Jiri spoke next: "I will go myself, with six Elves bearing glaives on me. I hope you brought some with you, Father."

Tiri replied with a grin: "Of course I did. You brought only bows, you fool."

Jiri sighed: "I've still got much to learn, Father. I will take three glaivesmen and three bowmen with me." Tiri grinned at his son.

Tirik and Mirak, so far merely observing, now took their turn to speak. "I will stay here and help out," said Mirak, while Tirik added: "I will take six miners with me to to assist you as best we can."

All nodded their agreement of the plan, before starting to leave, to gather the party.

Outside, in the camp, Malla'ak stood with his five bladirs and Liremir. Jiri came over with his small team, as did Irilie and an apparently far-too-eager Turuk. Tirik came to join them, with a rough looking bunch of male and female Demar people.

The squad was waved off as it set off along a forest path, concealed amongst the swamps, with Liremir leading them. The bulk of the forces then set out to face the enemy at the city gates.

In front of Arsac City, the massive combined army – of Humans, Demar, Svambar and Elves – were gathered at range, to assault the front. Scarlet, Tiri and Amarks took the lead, with Mirak behind them.

On a signal from Tiri, the Elven archers and Human spring-bolt bearers fired volley after volley upon the walls.

The troops defending dug down, and began to yell insults toward them. The volleys of arrows and bolts, onto the walls and gate, continued, as the combined army waited for their signal.

Behind Arsac City, on the Shaman's Path, the small entry team moved stealthily, with Liremir in front and Malla'ak right behind her. Turuk and Irilie were to their right, with Tirik following. The bladir were behind, along with the Elves. High guards were on the flanks, and the Demar miners brought up the rear. They moved slowly, following Liremir's footsteps. No words were said; only the subtle clinking of metal could be heard.

They crept slowly toward the secret passage, and saw no guards there. They hurried into a concealed corner to talk.

"I suggest we split up," said Jiri. "Tirik with me, to the gates; Malla'ak, Turuk and Irilie, lead your parties toward the hall – see if you can find anyone loyal to the new kingska."

They all nodded, and begin to make their way into the city – Jiri and Tirik moving off to the left; Malla'ak, Liremir, Turuk and Irilie taking their small party to the right.

Inside the Arsac City, toward the gates, Jiri and Tirik moved their team in silence, steering clear of patrols, and civilians in the nearby houses. Carefully, they made their way toward the gates, knowing fully that if they failed, the others already in the city would be located and killed.

They finally neared the gate, after who knew how long, where they saw warriors keenly guarding the gatehouse. Jiri signalled to Tirik, way behind him, to hold her position, as he sneaked closer with the Elves.

The guards appeared to be arguing over a last drumstick of

meat, and didn't see them coming. Arrows deftly flew, and the guards were skewered simultaneously in the throat, before Jiri and the glaives overran and finished them, spilling blood quickly. They hastened inside to get the gates open.

At roughly the same time, near the bladirs' barracks, Malla'ak, Liremir, Turuk and Irilie were making their way. To the right, it was a dangerous route, with continuous patrols all about the place. They sneaked as carefully as they could.

Liremir and Malla'ak led the team to the bladirs' barracks and pit, where a large number was gathered and preparing for training. They watched in silence for a moment, before, to all of their surprise, Malla'ak suddenly gave a mere nod, before rushing forward and hurling himself into the pit.

Poor Liremir could only follow as, once the momentary surprise had passed, the rest of the bladirs did the same. Turuk and Irilie followed them, but remained on the edge of the pit, peering over and ready to jump into the fray.

The voice of Malla'ak suddenly roared around the bladir barracks: "Fight false kingska! Me true! You follow me, die not."

The hundred bladirs in the pit, their weapons already drawn, then started to lower them. One of the soldiers, a young bladir, shouted back: "We told you dead. Me promise lead. You promise lead, me gather loyal; fight for you."

Malla'ak promised him: "You fight good, me give lead, Kraser. Die... not give."

Kraser had made his decision: "Me fight for kingska. Me gather strong warriors." With that, the young Svambar darted out of the pit. It wasn't long before the sounds of tussling, and blades smashing against metal, could be heard.

They were fighting in the pit's distance, clashing with

defectors who refused to resume loyalty. Many were killed in the pit, by Kraser and a growing number of followers, before the loyalists started moving into the barracks. Again, the noise of fighting was heard.

It was some while before Kraser once again reappeared, breathing heavily and covered in blood. Behind him, over two hundred bladirs were shouting victoriously: "We loyal true kingska! We fight with!"

Malla'ak climbed up onto the wall of the pit and yelled out: "Took ma, anvach!" At that, Malla'ak moved forward, with Liremir close behind him, their weapons drawn. The rest of the bladirs followed, as did Turuk and Irilie, with the four high guards in tow.

As they headed for the king's halls, all now firmly believed that they were going to win. Mud splashed on the nearby structures, as they picked up speed and rushed forth.

At roughly the same time, in front of Arsac city...

The arrows were still raining down, when the gates suddenly opened.

A shout from Scarlet sent the whole army charging: "Forward! Take these traitors down! Blood shall spill on this day; only one king shall stand!"

Scarlet joined the charge, closely followed by Amarks and Tiri. The High Guard, both on foot and mounts, weren't far behind, and the arkska followed suit, along with the handful of Elves armed with glaives. The rest of the combined army, led by Mirak, followed behind, providing long-range cover and backup, as they rushed the city gates. Enemy arkska, and the remaining handful of disloyal bladirs, rushed to engage them, and they clashed just metres from the gate.

Bodies started to drop on both sides. Some of the enemy were impaled, as the Demar miners sent earthen spikes into them. Bolts and arrows assaulted them from the sides, as the gateway became a chaotic battleground, both armies desperately pushing forth. None seemed to be gaining the upper hand.

Then, after a few minutes of brutal rough and tumble, a yell came out, from a defected Svambar sentry behind the defences: "It is a diversion! They are attacking the king's hall!"

The defending arkska and bladirs suddenly appeared a little rudderless, and as some seemed to consider pulling back, the protective mass began to lose its resolve; this proved to be a big mistake. Seeing them retreat and disband, the combined army – with Scarlet, Tiri and Amarks inspiring by example – pushed on mercilessly; the battle didn't last long after that. Before long, the enemy was completely split, some trying to get to the king's hall, while others fought back in vain.

While the mounting losses on both sides were huge, they were increasingly those of the enemy. Blood flowed freely into the swamps, turning the water red, and creating macabre patterns in the green of the swamps' detritus.

Scarlet, Tiri and Amarks rushed to support the attack on the king's halls, the High Guard and the Elves following; the rest of the army stayed behind to fight.

Tirik and her group emerged from the gate at that moment, greeting with a wave, as she passed, her allies rushing for the king's halls. Jiri followed behind her, from the gatehouse, and before long the streets were filled with soldiers of the Human, Svambar and Elven races.

The fighting became a massacre; it would be over in mere moments. The allied soldiers would then remain to gather the bodies of the dead – a task with which Mirak and the miners would stay to help.

Inside Arsac City, near the king's halls, just a few minutes earlier...

Malla'ak, Liremir, Turuk and Irilie – along with the loyalist bladirs and four high guards – were carrying out their surprise attack on the king's halls. The guarding warriors of the arkska, not expecting the covert assault, were quickly overrun, as bladirs, from the depths of the hall corridors, stormed forward to attack them; the elite fighters crashed into one another. Malla'ak was the first to engage.

"Cowards, you all!" he spat, furiously. "Not worthy my seat!"

Liremir, as always, was nearby, shooting short bursts of arrows at selected targets, to cover her master's back.

Turuk, still as eager as ever, threw herself right into the middle of the brawl, with Irilie and the High Guard behind her.

The battle was a brutal one, with casualties mounting on both sides. All were equally trained for battle, but each possessed his or her own warrior skills. All tactics were on display, fair or foul: dirt-throwing; fist-tossing, headbutting and even aiming between the legs with their longswords – it was an all-out battle between the strong and the weak. As the battle raged, a lone sentry hurried to the gates to alert the forces there – unknown to him, he was sealing their fate.

Being on the low ground, Malla'ak, Irilie and Turuk's forces were fighting an uphill battle. The blood flowed down past their feet, gathering at the bottom, as the body count rose; the ground became mud, as slippery as ice and drenched with blood. Each individual engagement lasted mere seconds, but the consequences were brutal. Blood sprayed all over; armours once grey, and surcoats once clean, were now red with the blood of the enemy. Gradually, more forces began to filter in from above.

Scarlet, Amarks and Tiri were hot on their tails, penning their foes in from behind. The Elves began to shoot their arrows, picking them off like fish in a barrel, as the High Guard pushed out to the flanks. The enemy were trapped in a slaughterhouse, but their warrior pride kept them there, fighting to the death; they would not run; there would be no surrender or retreat. Soon, the traitorous bladirs began to fall, one by one, as the pressure continued to build, to the extent that they could hold it off no longer; they were cut down where they stood.

Citizens hid in their houses, peeking cautiously through their windows, lest a stray arrow wander their way; all stayed hidden, as the battle raged.

While the High Guard and the loyalist bladirs fought the last of their enemies, Malla'ak, Liremir, Scarlet, Amarks, Turuk, Irilie, Tiri and Jiri pressed forth, into the king's halls. They were immediately struck by a rotten stench, emerging from within. Whatever was going on inside, and whoever was cooking it up, it smelled like the swamp, but more rotten, infused with the stench of bad herbs.

The group entered the king's main hall, to find a twisted, dark-green Svambar sitting on the throne, a Dark Elf beside him; nearby a dark figure stood, in a hooded robe.

Unexpectedly, at that moment, Silor came teleporting into the hall, to the surprise of all present. Then, in a calm and collected voice, he addressed them: "I'm sorry for my unannounced arrival; it seems that when you entered these halls, you broke a spell preventing me from doing the same."

He wandered toward the hooded figure. "This robed individual, us time mages believe, is one of the disciples of Miller, the time corruptor. I have attended, as the time mage watching over the Svambar people, to deal with this threat, and to find out who, why and how..."

The robed figure laughed out loud, apparently totally mad. "My master is the true master of time. You insolent little worms don't know what you are dealing with; you are weak and all will perish. We are the *true* order of time!"

Silor calmly mumbled something, under his breath, and in a fraction of a second he and the robed figure disappeared, teleported away from the king's hall, for a reason unknown.

The rest, initially in something a little resembling shock at these events, soon returned to the present situation. The false Svambar king rose and spoke: "Me mighty; you weak. Me take throne, you bow. We serve masters!"

Malla'ak, clearly furious at these words, raged back at him: "You not mighty; you weak! You old ways; weak ways. Me new ways; strong ways. Me challenge!" Malla'ak suddenly pointed his sword at the false king, the challenge unambiguous.

The false king ran at Malla'ak, who charged in return. Soon a battle was underway, fierce and filled with rage. Swords crashed against armour, but little else could be clearly made out, by even the quickest eye.

It was then that Tiri noticed the Dark Elf had disappeared. He suddenly spotted a dark-purple blade thrusting at Malla'ak, and hurled his dagger at the space behind it. There was a loud hiss, as the Dark Elf reappeared, enraged, Tiri's dagger embedded in his leg – he responded by ignoring the kingska and instead charging Tiri; Tiri returned the attack in kind. The speed of that brawl increased, until so fast that none except the Elves could bear witness to its ferocity. Jiri prepared to jump into the fight, but Tiri quickly raised a hand, warning his son to stay out of it.

Scarlet, Amarks, Turuk and Irilie were also keen to engage the false king, when suddenly Liremir stood tall, pointing her bow in their direction, loaded with six arrows; she stood between her master and the group. "Please stay out of the fight, as hard as it is to do. This is a battle for honour; a fight for the strongest. Whoever wins will earn honour and fame amongst the people. So, please keep out of it." There were a few grumbles but, if only for their own reputations, the group respected these words.

Fortunately, the fight was brutal and swift; within less than a minute, the false king lay dead, his head cut off. Malla'ak stood tall in his victory, though he was heavily injured. Liremir rushed over to help treat his wounds, careful not to enrage her master.

Tiri had himself spent the last minute beating down the Dark Elf, who was now motionless on the floor. But, Tiri did not escape unharmed; a deep, dark-purple wound was clearly seen by all, before he dropped like a sack of grain. Jiri rushed toward his father; he knew very well what had happened.

"Father, hold on, please!"

Tiri, weak and barely able to speak, responded: "Son, please, there is nothing you can do; the Dark Elf's poison has left its traces in my blood. I feel closer to nature now.

"Do not hate them for this. I still believe there is a way to save them from service to their masters; they are still kin to us – remember that."

And, with those words, Tiri, the great king of peace, died. Jiri's cries could be heard from miles away.

It is here that I think we shall once again bring Liremir's diary to life, for what followed was an event so sad, yet so happy, it is worthy of note:

> *"And, so it was that the Great Elven King of Peace, the saviour of his people, died. His body was collected on a bed of leaves and sticks, to carry him home with all haste, to be buried. As part of the slaves' honour*

law, I was given permission to return with them, to mourn the loss of my king; my master left in the care of a young shaman called Asaiks.

"A war meeting was immediately set, to take place at the Human capital two months later, in order to discuss these events, and to discover what the time mages knew of them. Then, all departed for home, to bury the dead and mourn their losses.

"The Elven ceremony for the hyr was special. Silir, the leader of the Druids, spoke words of praise and achievement, and said a long prayer, that he may meet his ancestors in the woods beyond, and that they may watch over his people and guide them. In our native tongue, these words were so full of meaning, yet are very rarely said. The hyr was wrapped in a cloak, made of the finest materials the forest could provide, along with his most personal belongings, then taken to be buried underneath a very special young tree which grows in the middle of the forest – it is from the seed of the old Kings' Tree, in our former home. Tiri would be the first king to lie in this spot and watch over his people's new home.

"When he was buried, Jiri, our vingara, was asked to step up in front of the people and kneel. At that very ceremony, a crown of leaves and sticks, very old and preserved by the will of the forest, was placed upon his head; his father's sword, Ariski, was hung around his waist. The cry went out: 'Where one hyr lies, another shall rise!' The forest protects and guides Tiri now, as do his ancestors.

"Six days of silent mourning followed, where only eating was allowed, but no manual labour. To mourn the loss of a great hyr, I remained for six days with my people, keeping my adopted father company, before I left to return to my master.

"By now worried sick for him, I ran most of the way to Svambar. Luckily, when I returned, he was recovering well. I stayed by his side, not leaving it until the war meeting was to convene."

And, so it was that, roughly a month and a half later, they all travelled with a personal escort to the Human capital, to discuss how next to fight this threat. In Grassiak, the leaders gathered in the throne room at King's Manor, each with a handful of personal guards outside.

Jiri, still in mourning at losing his father, was accompanied by Silir and a younger female beside her. Malla'ak was wounded, yet still stubborn enough to stand, with Liremir close by; the new lead shaman Ariski, and the bladirs' leader Kraser were also beside him. They dominated one side of the big table, in front of which stood Scarlet, Amarks, Turuk and Irilie.

The Demar people's council were there, alongside the time mages, Larue, Larus, Iksas and Silor – the latter looking quite badly wounded and barely able to stand, supported by his staff.

Coughing slightly at times, Silor spoke up: "Sorry to make it so brief; that fight with the corrupted time mage took quite the effort – but I can gladly say that he is safely under lock and key at our tower.

"We have discovered that the enemy is massing forces in Barlar. However, due to a lack of specific information about where, how many or whom, I suggest we don't hurry there quite yet. I have heard that some of the Corrupted Elves are starting to rebel against their masters, and I believe it may be wise to try making contact with them; I propose that we travel down there to deal with the Corrupted Elves first."

Silor suddenly started to cough blood into a handkerchief, and Larus quickly took a hold of him, teleporting the two of them away without a word.

Knowing the narrative, Larue continued on his behalf: "I'm sorry we all have to see Brother Silor this way; he was quite badly injured. To continue, we have seen signs of a twisted ritual taking place in Sedrak. We don't know what it is, but we are certain that it isn't good. Therefore, we recommend sending a smaller party to investigate and, if necessary, deal with the matter; the main combined armies will rally around Barlar, and ensure safety on that border."

The gathering nodded their agreement.

Scarlet now started to speak: "I suggest we select two to lead the party, and that each race has a representative. The remainder will organize border defence and gathering our armies in preparation for war. However, it is my firm belief that we should go farther than simply gathering each of the races' defences to fight side-by-side; I think we should form a combined army, one which follows the command of a council, represented by each race's leadership. This army will, in turn, be utilized as a force against threats to any of our member races; our own domestic armies can be used for our own individual needs. Each member will wear the same armour as they have done previously, but with uniform surcoats to represent the alliance." She looked around her for agreement.

Amarks nodded, expanding on Scarlet's suggestion. "The idea is solid, as I'm sure you can all tell. And, furthermore, as well as the armies, we can share military tactics and training, developing greater elite warfare than any we would achieve by ourselves; we can ensure that no one will have the ability to threaten our lives any more, in our own lands. This coming war may shape the future of this land. If we do not stand together, how are we ever to defend against a larger enemy?"

Malla'ak responded to the proposal without hesitating: "One warrior be strong; many be stronger. Me approve. Me wish all gather strong warriors, one all."

Jiri nodded his agreement, as he replied: "It is a great plan, indeed. I shall present it to our people and we shall see how many volunteer to participate. As you all know, we Elves have no standing army, but we can call on Elves to defend ourselves, when necessary."

Romboka engaged in the conversation now, having been

whispering among the rest of his council. "We have many young Demar men and women, who wish to go out to explore. I think that if the council proposes this to our people, we can send numbers of them for support. Yes, we will join this combined army."

Larue nodded his approval at the overwhelming universal agreement, and spoke his mind: "The time mages may not number many, but in time we will join you, and we will start to train new time mages, to further our existence."

Scarlet once again spoke up, before anyone else had the chance: "Then, I propose that Kingska Malla'ak and King Jiri lead this small party, sending ten in total to support.

"I also propose naming our combined army 'The Selection Army'. It is a simple name, but it is appropriate. This small party would then be named 'The First Selection Group'."

There followed an increasing murmur of approval; clearly, all were in agreement with her suggestion.

Looking them all over, Jiri spoke: "If we are all in agreement, then I say that we conclude the meeting, and return home to inform our people. Then, in two months' time, the First Selection Group will meet at the Crossroads, in Rroker, with ten men and women from each race, representative of their leaders. Those who wish to be part of the group should gather here, as it is close to Barlar and provides easy access."

All of them nodded to denote their respect, and raised their bows in camaraderie, before starting to leave the throne room – each to their own, for now.

In the Elven city of Earasira, a few days later, the Elves were gathered around the king's home, waiting patiently for news from their new hyr.

After what seemed an age, Jiri and Silir finally came outside, to be greeted by their people. Jiri wore full ceremonial dress, of the finest leaves and his crown. Silor was in her finest robe. As Jiri raised his hand, silence followed. He spoke clearly and proudly to his people, in their native tongue.

"Grefyih tar porple. Amer, alleice gran valantaar, fuor unert Aromiror Porple."

The short, yet perfect speech caused the people to applaud and celebrate their king; their wise and all-knowing young hyr.

A feast was underway, to celebrate the new relationships, and in the knowledge that it would be the last meal in this city for some. Simple food, yet so appetizing, was presented before them on the finest plates of stone. Jugs of beautiful wood were filled with water and herb-based refreshments, provided by the forest. Animals, blessed by Druids after being shot, had been dressed and were now cooking over a blazing fire, which the Elves danced around, as they feasted and enjoyed what nature provided; they danced to the music made by instruments crafted from the forest. It was a happy day, yet also a sad one, as many were leaving to join the combined army, knowing that they might not return alive. For now, though, peace ruled the Golden Forest, the home of the Elves. Soon, bloody times would await them.

A day later, in the Human capital of Grassiak, the people of the city and beyond were gathered outside the inner wall, waiting for their queen and king to appear; eager for news of the war, and what was being done to keep them safe.

Atop the walls, above the gate, Scarlet and Amarks appeared, in their finest cloth. Beside them was Turuk, also finely dressed. Irilie stood next to them, in full ceremonial white armour, standing proud and tall, as she kept them safe.

The people began to roar, clapping and cheering the royal couple. Some shouted: "Long live the queen! Long live the king!"

Harry, the old herald for her father and mother, and now for Scarlet, sounded a horn, before he called to the crowd: "Silence! The king and queen wish to inform their people of news for the kingdom!"

Scarlet stepped forward alongside Amarks, to a cheer from the crowd. As she raised her hand, silence followed. She spoke calmly, yet in the tone of a leader. "My people – *our* people – today, we can finally announce news which we hope and believe will keep us safe for many years to come. As you already know, we have an alliance standing, between Humans, Elves, Demar and Svambar people. Today, that alliance is coming to greater fruition. We have agreed to form a combined army, which will be known as the 'Selection'. Any among you who wishes to join this army, report to myself or King Amarks; we personally handle recruitment for this, along with other leaders or representatives, who ensure our people's safety.

"You may ask why this venture has become necessary. We have learnt that the enemy gathers at Barlar. We are going to defend the border there, to ensure that they don't attack us unprepared."

Amarks stepped forward, with a rather short speech: "Our people, please understand that we wish the best for you. But, if our army is busy elsewhere, then who will defend our beloved lands? Therefore, I humbly beg you to sign up and allow us to relieve our army, to ensure the safety of the citizens, without the need to be in a perpetual state of war."

The people cheered again at these words. Many were already calling out: "I'll join the Selection, my queen and king!"

Irilie stepped forward, raising her hand to dim the shouting yell. "Then, let the gates be opened, and the people permitted to sign up!"

The inner gates opened, to a bustling queue of men and women, lining up and desperate to join; many simply returned to their day to day life. The High Guard checked all that were volunteering, ensuring they were unarmed and safe to be permitted inside the city gates. Scarlet, Amarks, Turuk and Irilie watched on.

Irilie turned to them: "Well, this went better than I thought, my queen and king."

Amarks nodded; "It did, indeed. Which is why we have a personal instruction for you, Irilie."

Irilie turned to Amarks and knelt, with a bow. "Whatever my queen and king command of me."

Scarlet spoke in a commanding tone: "High Captain, you are to personally gather five high guards and five soldiers to keep Princess Turuk safe; we charge you both with representing us at the First Selection Group."

Turuk was immediately excited, and stood to jump for joy. Irilie partly rose at that, suddenly forcing the girl back down to her knees. Scarlet and Amarks watched the disciplining of their child, without intervention.

After shooting a stern look at Turuk, who was now frozen in fear, Irilie replied: "My squire and I are very honoured to bestow this task. I shall ensure the safety of my squire, Princess Turuk, myself. I shall leave my ten best to guard you, one among them whom I believe is worthy to take over my position one day. She may be a squire now, but her potential is big."

Scarlet nodded firmly, signalling them both to stand, which they did.

Amarks told Irilie: "We are happy that you would leave such

fine people behind; we see that choosing you for High Captain was wise. We shall watch closely the squire to which you refer; if she is the one we believe her to be, it will be interesting to see what becomes of her progress. Now, go about your orders, High Captain."

Irilie bowed once more, as did Turuk, eager never to again be disciplined by Irilie in front of her mother and father. They then left, with great haste, to their task.

In the Svambar capital of Arsac, the Svambar people had barely recovered from the brutal fighting, and the loss of so many warriors. All were now gathered in front of the King's Halls, waiting for their new kingska to speak.

Malla'ak appeared in full fighting uniform, Liremir kneeling to his side, and slightly behind him, also fully armed and equipped for battle. As the people stood silently, out of respect for their leader, Malla'ak spoke:

"My people, you strong; survived. We fight; join the Selection Army: combined allies' army. Only strong go. Ten strong, follow me, journey First Selection Group. Pits all who fight!"

After the address, most of the people went about their business again, scared of another war and how many more would be lost. But, the warrior-minded among them rushed to the training pits of the bladirs, to be allowed to free their inner warrior, and prove themselves worthy to join the combined army. Even many arkska and bladirs put themselves forward.

Later, Malla'ak and Liremir came into the pits to watch the recruitment, Liremir keeping a hand near her dagger, always wary of traitors wishing to harm her master. People gathered in numbers, all of them eager to fight. Kraser stood in the middle of the pits, calling people forth, just as Malla'ak and Liremir arrived to watch.

"Twenty fighters at time," Kraser explained. "Fighters fight – last stand win; ten last standing strong. Rest weak!"

Twenty volunteers quickly started to fill the pit, and Kraser moved to the side. As he raised his one-handed sword, the fight began. No weapons were used – fists only, to prove those most strong and those who were weak. The fights were brutal; noses were bleeding and limbs broken as the day dragged on. One by one, the candidates fell.

When only one stood, Kraser signalled him over. The unsuccessful volunteers were then moved aside – some dragged unconscious – before the next twenty jumped in, preparing once again to be whittled down to one. And so, the process continued, until ten had been chosen; hundreds lay bleeding around the edges of the pit.

Malla'ak seemed amused at the sight, standing to clap those still standing, gleefully. "You ten strong warriors. Yes, Kraser sees. You follow me journey. Prepare; equip."

Kraser nodded, immediately taking the ten victors along to the armourer, to equip them. The rest, following any treatment, formed lines to sign up, hoping they were still worthy to do so.

Waiting for Kraser to return, Malla'ak dragged Liremir back to the halls, to kill some time.

A day later, in the throne hall of the Demar mine...

The council stood on the elevated rock, facing the stone throne in the centre, while the Demar people had gathered around the hall, curious about what they were to say.

Romboka rose from the throne, to speak to his fellow miners.

"Miners, today I bring news – news of danger to our lifestyle and to our trade. I have been told that the enemy gathers in the land of Barlar, which is very close to our own land. To counter their threat, our allies have put together a combined army, with a simple name: 'The Selection'. We have been asked to join this army, but as you know we are mere miners. Still, any of you who are willing to leave the mine and join the Selection can do so, with my blessing. You may join them in the Humans' capital city of Grassiak. I believe this may be an opportunity for you youngsters eager to leave the mine and go exploring.

"Mirak and Tirik will also be gathering a party of ten miners to assist in a critical mission, with other leaders and allies, to form what shall be known as the First Selection Group. If any of you wish to participate in this mission, report to them.

"That is all we have to say. Rock, guide us and be our soul."

The Demar people started to filter out of the vast room, whispering between each other. A handful of miners were hurrying over to Mirak and Tirik, evidently eager to sign up for the group, while the rest slowly disappeared, with their lamps and their candles, back into the dark mineshafts, making their way home or back to work, mining whatever the mountain may provide. A good number of the young ones, though, were already packing their belongings, ready to leave for their new life in the Selection Army.

And, so it was that the Selection came into being – without my help, it seems.

The next few weeks were spent training and preparing the small party to depart for the mission, while at the same time growing numbers came from all over to join the Selection: Elves, Demar, Svambar and Humans, together in one army. All classes of soldier enlisted, from the elite to the most amateur.

It was difficult for the Elves, many not keen to leave their beautiful forest. The Svambar only sent the strongest warriors – those tested in the pit. The Demar came in fewer numbers, but they were young and eager; even a member of their council put himself forward to enlist. The Humans provided the most recruits, though that was expected, since they didn't set such restrictive criteria regarding their recruitment.

And so, when the first Selection Army gathered, it went thus...

Chapter Six

The First War for the Land Between Times

The Crossroads, at Rroker.

Malla'ak and Liremir, in full armour and equipment, came walking alongside their group, from the direction of the roads to Svaplar. Turuk, Irilie and their group came from the roads to Grarss, while Jiri and his group of Elven archers came via the roads which led to the Golden Forest. Tirik and Mirak, along with a band of young miners, came trekking from the road to the Demar mines. They met up with each other at the midway point, all nodding their greetings, knowing that the journey was only just beginning.

Malla'ak was the first to speak. "Gather today, we. A journey begins."

Tirik and Mirak, already in good spirits, laughed at his turn of phrase. "Indeed so," grinned Tirik.

Mirak added: "Yes, we are finally going to arms. Stupid rules about peaceful miners..."

Jiri looked at them, a little worry passing over his expression. "Maybe so, but we must be careful; the journey is long and full of danger."

At that, Turuk spoke out, rather eagerly: "I hope we get to kill plenty."

Irilie smacked her on top of her helmet, with a hard hand,

wearing a grey-white glove, trimmed with silver. "That is no way for a noble nor a squire to speak – and especially not a princess! Behave, or I will make you." Turning her attention away from the pouting girl, Irilie turned to King Jiri: "Indeed, there is no knowing how many of us will return from this journey. We trek through hot sand in an unknown land – who knows how far without water?"

All nodded at those words, while Turuk just grumbled.

Malla'ak signalled for all to move out.

And, so the journey began. None knew what awaited them in the distance, nor how imminently.

The journey took the party through Rroker, to the northern edge of the Golden Forest. On the first evening, the First Selection Group made their camp there; tents were erected, rations were inspected and meat, which had been hunted earlier in the day, was cooked and eaten as they socialized, all taking effort to get to know one another better.

Jiri sat with Liremir and Malla'ak, alongside Turuk and Irilie, while Tirik and Mirak sat opposite them, around the middle campfire. They talked and ate heartily, Malla'ak, as always, the first to initiate conversation: "Strong ones await. Not know what face."

Jiri nodded, sharing the look of concern. "Indeed so; this is the unexpected. We expect we will face heat but, after that, who knows?"

Turuk hurried to chew on a mouthful of meat, so she could speak: "Let's hope not too many us are dead before we get the chance to fight."

While some sniggered, Irilie looked at Turuk with a sigh. "Squire, it is not always about killing; being wise, smart and strong is what makes a true leader. Your mother learned that the hard way, as she had to grow into doing that which was carried out by the former king and queen, when both died of an illness we could not treat. She had to man up, as her father told her, and do what was needed to lead her people. A weak ruler would have resulted in an uprising amongst the people, taking their demands by force. But, those rebels are under control, thanks to your mother possessing the necessary leadership skills in the most testing of times."

Still, Turuk grumbled as she ate, shooting an impetuous glare at Irilie.

Liremir sat quietly, listening as she wrote everything she could think of in her diary. Malla'ak was looking at her, and he chuckled.

"Slave write down mighty story," he said, with something which may have been pride. "Slave be good. Slave record all."

Liremir smiled at her master, and replied: "Yes, Master. Slave thought it was a good idea to record our adventure, so that others may know of it in the future. You are the greatest of all kings which have lived among the Svambar."

Malla'ak chuckled again at this, while the rest of the group looked on them with amusement.

After eating and relaxing, they all began to yawn in the falling darkness.

Jiri suggested: "Let's call it a night, and be fresh to travel tomorrow. It's going to be a long journey across the Golden Forest and Sandler. Beware, we have seen giant snakes and spiders on that route. We call the spiders 'erelaks', which really just means 'huge spiders'. The snakes we call 'amarask': 'terror snakes'; our scouts report them to be as tall as a tree."

The group listened, some now eager to hunt and fight the snakes, others more frightened by this than they cared to let on.

Shortly, they headed for their tents, and got some sleep for tomorrow. The following day they would rise early, and their travels would start over again, all knowing that the coming month or two spent travelling across Sandler might be slow going or a sprint, depending on the heat of the sun, and the eventfulness of their journey.

Two weeks later, the Elves had managed to guide the first Selection Army through the northern Golden Forest.

It had been a quiet and laborious few weeks, with not much of interest having happened – a positive, of course. The travelling was slow, with all their belongings and equipment, but they made progress. Fortunately, it was cool under the natural forest roof, the sun kept from the shadows.

They were all aware of the danger which lurked – but the question was where. All were secretly wary of the big snakes and spiders reported, yet had seen no signs of any yet.

As the days passed by, the end of the forest drew ever nearer, and the sand closer. Then, one day, near to the end, a loud *hiss* could be heard from the distance.

The First Selection Group froze, immediately holding. On command from their respective leaders, each unit assumed defensive positions. The High Guard and Svambar warriors formed an outer defence, led by Malla'ak, Irilie and Turuk; the miners and Elves, supported by spring-loaded gunners, made up the inner defence, with Jiri, Tirik, Mirak and Liremir alongside.

All looked around, trying to remain composed and locate whatever it was that had made the sound. They all already knew. It wasn't long before it revealed itself.

The snake was vast, resembling something between a large anaconda and a giant king cobra snake. It came sliding in from behind, at high speed, poised to attack.

Jiri barely managed to yell out the command, his throat was so instantly dry; "Amarask! Range, open fire!"

Shot after shot was fired; bolts, arrows and small rocks were all sent rocketing toward the amarask. It was immediately hit many times, all over, but nothing slowed its pace.

Irilie yelled out from the back: "High Guard, stand firm! Form a wall!" Between them, Irilie, Turuk and the High Guard formed an impenetrable wall of pointed longswords and halberds, as the amarask came crashing into them – most were sent flying backward from the impact.

Never one to be left out of the fray, Malla'ak yelled out: "Warriors, attack! Down take!" He charged in, with his elite warriors behind him, and they hurled themselves through the air at the snake – in return, the amarask swatted them aside with its tail, like insects.

The serpent reared up to attack Malla'ak, when suddenly an arrow plunged into its head, making it withdraw in pain, as Liremir roared in victory: "I've got your back, Master!"

Malla'ak, too busy to reply, hacked at the snake with his longsword in one hand, desperately trying to defend with the other holding his one-handed weapon.

Mirak and Tirik formed a giant boulder of the earth, sticks and anything else in sight, and proceeded to hurl it at the snake's head. The impact was a surprisingly hard clump, dazing the serpent, which hissed madly in return.

Turuk, encouraged by this opportune moment, charged in with her halberd raised high, and speared the creature in the throat, yelling out in glory. "Someone take its head off, before it gets me!" she then screamed.

Malla'ak ran toward it, dropping the one-handed sword to the ground and lunging a powerful uppercut with the longsword, plunging it into the beast's throat, just below the protruding halberd.

Blood flowed freely from the wounds, and the snake began to writhe and hiss in agony. Jiri offered a short prayer to the Forest gods, before sending an arrow into the throat; the amarask died quickly.

"That was one tough snake," Jiri panted, as Turuk pulled out her halberd with a smile, covering herself with blood in the process.

"That was fun," she said. "Where can we find another one?"

Irilie, clearly annoyed by the comment, grabbed the girl by the neck of her armour, dragging her away while she struggled and protested.

Malla'ak picked up his one-handed sword and raised it high. "Won! Strong, we. Treat injured, slave."

Liremir rushed over and immediately started to treat the wounded. Luckily, none had been hurt too badly, protected by their robust builds and the armour they wore. The High Guard's superior armour saved the day for them, and their sore ribs would not hinder their standing to march on.

The Elves set to skinning the snake, offering its body on a fire to nature, thankful for it giving its life in exchange for theirs.

Once all of the wounded were checked for restrictive injuries, and the ritual of respect carried out for the amarask, they moved out, resuming their journey into Sandler. What else would await them in this desert land, only time and nature could know.

They reached Sandler on the northern edge, and the journey across the hot and arid land of sand began.

The Elves were immediately tasked with scouting, and the miners with using their expertise to locate water. The rest kept guard.

For those wearing armour of metal, only a simple layer of clothing protected the wearer from the scorching heat. Water became an issue almost immediately.

Hindered by the gear they wore and carried, as day by day passed, they walked slower and slower. Their water rations were dwindling quickly; within a month, it had almost all gone, and still they were only halfway across the desert.

"So hot," Turuk gasped. "So thirsty."

Irilie shared some water with her, agreeing: "We need to find water now; we're going to run out. This heat is killing us." She glanced over at Liremir, badly dehydrated, due to giving all of her water over to her master, who himself looked surprisingly better refreshed than everyone else.

Jiri shared the concern, calling out: "Tirik and Mirak, still no sign of water? We have almost run out."

Tirik replied tiredly – tired of the heat and of being asked: "Not in the slightest."

Mirak added: "Only small pools of it, as far we can see."

Not happy with the news, Malla'ak yelled: "Water! Warriors weak without. Need water!"

They all just looked at him, while Liremir gently began stroking his chin. "Easy, Master. Save your strength. Be strong among the weak." This seemed to calm Malla'ak for the moment.

Over the sandy dunes they saw what appeared to be riders, approaching at high speed. Immediately, the tired and partly dehydrated group formed a defensive wall, all apprehensive at what and who was coming toward them.

The riders stopped a few metres in front of them, and they all faced each other, silently. Then, one of riders strode forward, slowly, and called out: "You look like those who have run out of water. My name is Kalip. I am a trader, who has set up three water posts in these lands. Plenty of treasure hunters pass through here, hoping to find something of worth in these desert lands."

Knowing how hot-headed Malla'ak could be, Jiri made sure he got in first, yelling back at the stranger: "We are the First Selection Group of the combined races. We are travelling to Sedrak on a mission. We will trade payment of iron coins in exchange for water."

The rider known as Kalip answered: "If all races are combining for a mission, it must be important. I will make you a deal: five silver per litre of water from my trading post. It's the least I can do to aid you in such an important mission. Please, follow me."

Jiri replied, good-naturedly: "Thank you for such a good deal. We will gladly take it. It is good to see some traders have a kind heart." He signalled for the rest to follow him, as they moved toward Kalip and followed him to his trading post.

They arrived there after a gruelling four hours, with the sun baking them the whole time. When they arrived, Kalip directed them to a water butt, where they quickly refilled their containers. Then, Malla'ak, Liremir, Jiri, Tirik, Mirak, Turuk and Irilie all followed Kalip to a small hut nearby.

Kalip sat down at a table, taking a drink, as the rest stood before him. Shortly, a man entered, whispering into Kalip's ear, who nodded and looked at them. "Right, the price will be seventy iron coins for the water."

The party glanced at each other expectantly, before collecting between them the iron coins, and putting them on the table. Kalip counted the money and nodded. "So, that concludes our deal. I will give you a map of my trading post, to take with you, so that when you return, you can find water."

Kalip placed a map onto the table, which Jiri took and folded, nodding gratefully. "Thank you. May the forest and time guide you."

As they stepped outside, they gathered the waiting troops together, and prepared to set off.

Suddenly, a dust cloud filled with horses and men came bowling into the trading post. Kalip instantly came running out of the hut, and on seeing the rushing party, yelled out fearfully: "Sand bandits are attacking! Guards, keep my hut safe. Protect the water!"

The First Selection Group unhesitantly started to form a defensive line. It would be a quick fight.

Chapter Seven
A Ritual Uncovered

The next month and a half dragged by, and they made a quick stop at another of Kalip's trading posts on the way. The heat was relentless.

Then, finally, they saw water, from the top of a sand dune.

Turuk excitedly cried out: "I see water, and plenty of it!" An entire small sea and archipelago sat before them.

Irilie came running over to her, slapping her atop the helmet. "Easy, squire; calm yourself. Don't just rush ahead, now."

Tirik and Mirak were also cautious, carefully looking on. Malla'ak would look at the sight before them – the end of the desert – and would certainly be happy that the real journey could now begin.

Jiri, on the other hand, spotted something which signalled danger to him: "I see dark clouds, people. This doesn't look good at all. I'd bet this is made by whoever we are dealing with down there."

Liremir, looking on, suddenly called out: "There appears to be a road of sorts, through the middle of the seas, look." She pointed out what was little more than a dirt track, and they all appeared surprised when they saw it, not having been aware of its being there.

"That isn't a natural path, that's for sure," said Jiri. "Let's move in for a closer look. Weapons at the ready; don't let your guards down now."

They all started to follow Jiri down to the dirt road, extra careful now, with an increasing sense that something about this all seemed off. Why was the path here, and who made it? The First Selection Group was about to find out.

They arrived watchfully at the dirt road, bordering Sedrak and Sandler. Tirik, Mirak and the miners immediately started to check the area, to make sure it was safe. Once the all-clear to go was given, they moved slowly.

High guards stepped alongside Svambar warriors, with Malla'ak, Turuk and Irilie next to them. Jiri, Liremir, Tirik and Mirak led the rest of the group behind them. All had their weapons drawn, ready to fight at a moment's notice. Tension was high, and with it the fear of a surprise attack.

The day seemed to move slower than usual, with barely any small-talk. The level of anxiety rose, as the hours passed; not one of the group sheathed their swords. The rest bore their axes, maces, halberds, arrows, bolts, or even held stones.

As the day gradually ground to a halt, the sky became more and more black – so dark, in fact, that within the hour of the sun setting, there was no light at all, other than the two torches lit by the group. An eerie howl in the distance, then a giant splash, made the group jump and look around them, but there was nothing to be seen. Only the commands from their leaders, and their disciplined training, was controlling the soldiers' resolve.

They camped for the night with no fire and no tents – only sleeping skins and dried meat, formed for quick response, with heavy armour to the sides, protecting the rest in the middle.

The darkness never seemed to move away; sleep came slowly, and was interrupted quickly. None slept much, the fear of attack, and whatever lurked in the waters keeping them awake and alert. Liremir shook with fear most of the night, mumbling incoherently in her brief moments of sleep, having already curled beneath her master's feet.

The cold set in, later in the evening, and it was a struggle for all to keep warm. Because of the sparse, dirt surroundings, there was little shelter to be made of the earth.

The next morning revealed the consequences of the cold night, as the group discovered that two spring-loaded bow gunners had died from the cold, as well as a miner and a Svambar warrior. The Elves, more naturally built to withstand, had all survived for now. They sombrely packed up their belongings and tossed the dead unceremoniously into the lake – the only suitable burial which could be afforded them.

Then, they moved on. There was no time to mourn the dead, nor to bury them properly. Time was wasting, and war drew closer.

They moved with stiff steps, their fear high, and the agony of cold joints bothering them all – but they could not stop to treat themselves; they simply had to move on. The days dragged on, day after day, of the same fear and anxiety, ever higher than before.

In the days which followed, two more Svambar warriors fell, and another miner and a Human died; the group now grew ever smaller. The inevitable question was by now starting to cross all of their minds: should they turn back and call the mission a failure? They all knew, of course, that they couldn't. They had to succeed or die trying – there was simply no other way; their journey must end in any way other than failure.

At this point, they saw a small island near the path, and decided to explore it. Drawing closer, they came across a small lake of clear water, and what looked to be a pleasant and tranquil camping site. Although not quite yet ready to call it a day, they decided to make camp here, if only to replenish some morale.

Small sticks were gathered from nearby willow-like trees, and that night spirits were lifted, with a small fire to cook on. They cooked simple rations, eating and talking if only to try forgetting the miserable situation they were in – for just a brief moment. They each bedded down that night with better morale than at any time in the past month, raising their tents to shield them from nature.

But, that was certainly about to shatter. The next morning, as they were eating breakfast and preparing to set out, the sky erupted in a strike of thunder and lightning. The sky grew dark suddenly – unnaturally so.

A shout went out to get into defensive positions, and the order was quickly put into effect, as rain began hammering down, thunder and lightning striking around them. The morale which had renewed so effectively quickly began to diminish.

And, in the glow of each lightning strike in the darkness, an otherworldly creature appeared in silhouette: it could only be described as a wolf with the long body of a snake.

So terrifying was the apparition that the troops began to scream in pure panic; the fear set in hard. The leaders rallied desperately, trying to maintain order and confidence, but they were every bit as frightened.

All, that was, except for Malla'ak.

The Svambar king stood before the beast, raising his weapons, and roared at the top of his voice: "Challenge me, monster sea! You not scary; you weak! Me strong! *Me* scary!"

Liremir, shaking and barely standing, stood dutifully behind her master, vowing to keep him safe, even if she was so frightened she could barely shoot straight.

The cold was setting in hard, as rain slammed down from above; all were drenched through and struggling to retain heat. The water was creating waves which crashed against the edges of the island, as the wind kicked up in strength.

The creature disappeared and reappeared continuously in the lightning storm, appearing at different spots all over the island. Fear, anxiety and paranoia among the group increased, the longer it went on. Moments – mere minutes – began to feel like hours, even though time was flying past them. Increasingly tense, the Human spring-loaded gunners reacted to the pressure, and began firing randomly into the storm, wasting ammo in fits of panic. Then, ignoring the yelled orders of Irilie and Turuk, they fled in terror, into the darkness. Irilie and Turuk cursed them, though the High Guard still stood firm. All was not looking good.

The creature suddenly presented itself in full form, circling the island, its dark-grey skin covered in scales. The dreadful beast looked to be at least two or three metres in length. With the rain pelting down, against the backdrop of thunder and lightning strikes, it presented a terrifying and formidable sight.

Jiri quickly ordered all of the Elves to open fire, carefully and with judgement. Still, only half of the arrows hit their target. The younger Elves, none of whom had ever seen battle, were so scared that their shots strayed way off target; the older archers, more familiar with war conditions, aimed and shot more steadily.

Liremir was failing to hit anything, her own shots going wayward, as she screamed out in terror and frustration. Malla'ak grabbed her by her armour, lifting her up and tossing her into the mud. He towered over her, yelling in her face: "Slave not hit. Beat slave! Slave bad guard. Replace; useless!"

Liremir, now even more afraid of her master than of the fearful creature, knelt in the mud and stood up, now taking more careful aim. With composure, and fearful of Malla'ak's rejection and degradation, her shots began to hit.

Jiri was looking around him, taking curious note of the pattern of the waves splashing against the island. Then, he quickly shouted to Irilie: "Get the rest of your group to surround the small pond. It is somehow connected to the splashing of the bigger lake."

Irilie didn't argue; "Got it. All on me!" Irilie, the high guards and Turuk formed a circle around the smaller pond.

Jiri then yelled: "Svambar, create a lot of distraction; make noise and wave your weapons. Elves, keep the arrows flying, but gradually fall farther and farther back."

Malla'ak stood up and roared, beating his weapon on his shoulders. *"Ake Svambar Irke, Warca. Warraga, ma vach!"* The Svambar warriors followed suit, repeating his mantra; the noise of yelling heard even over the thunder and lightning.

The Elves fired, even as they retreated slowly backward, their fear still on the cusp of taking them over as they did so.

Now clearly angered, the sea monster circled the island again, making strange squeals and screams in the air – a noise capable of freezing all that heard it.

The rain still came down in huge volume, thunder, lightning and the tumultuous waves pummelling the island. It felt like they were in a trap; that they were going to sink. Meanwhile, the creature appeared to have managed to circle them, by diving underneath the road they were on; they realized there must be tunnels underneath them. It felt like hours before the monster emerged, flying through the middle pond with horrific screeching.

The Humans quickly stabbed at it, with their halberds and longswords, as the Elves fired their arrows and the miners hurled massive rocks. It squealed in pain from every impact, as Malla'ak and the Svambar warriors leapt onto its back, hacking away at it with their weapons. It writhed and tossed several of the warriors, as it desperately attempted retreat into the water.

But, Jiri was quicker than the beast, and within four steps he buried his sword in its throat. Blood poured out of it, as it writhed with even greater intensity, tossing Malla'ak and the last of the warriors to the ground. Then, it fell with a boom, almost crushing Irilie, who quickly leapt out of the way.

After checking that the creature was dead, they dragged it up out of the water to exam it. Then they looked about them, to find and treat their wounded. They found that two more Svambar warriors had been lost, and that the last remaining spring-loaded gunners had fled, and were likely dead.

What was this beast? Who on the earth had brought it here? The questions were left unanswered for now, as they began to gather up their belongings and leave; the journey had to go on, and time was running out.

*

They travelled for almost another month, before stumbling on a large piece of land, which looked anything but natural. Tirik, Mirak and the miners checked it over to confirm it was safe. Once clear, the rest of the group were called over, to investigate for themselves.

Another day came to a halt, as they made camp near a wooded area of strange appearance. They set up a giant tent which, once erect, the leaders would enter to talk, plan and strategize a concerted course of action, should they encounter another enemy – if any further dared show themselves.

Malla'ak, Liremir, Jiri, Irilie, Turuk, Mirak and Tirik stood around a table constructed in the huge tent, all peering down at a map they had compiled from what the miners, Mirak and Tirik could make out from the ground.

Jiri was the first to speak: "I think this is the best map we are going to get, from what I can see. I and my Elves should scout on ahead, and you follow closely nearby; let's see if we can find out whoever is making this mess."

Turuk spoke ahead of Irilie: "Wise idea, indeed. Still, let's hope there is more than just this, and that a good fight lies ahead." Irilie nodded her approval of Turuk's words.

Malla'ak pointed at the map as he spoke: "There, line form warriors – strong place."

They all glanced down, to find that it appeared Malla'ak had spotted a small hillside, near where they were moving to. Liremir was smiling, proud to serve a master so wise.

Tirik suggested: "We can scale the hill, to make it easier to defend."

Mirak added: "And, we can make earth spikes, so it is harder to follow us up."

Irilie nodded, gratefully; "That would be helpful, indeed. Can you also make walls for us to hide behind, in case the enemy is there? The Svambar warriors can draw their attention, with your aid and that of the Elves."

They all nodded their agreement. Jiri once again took the mantle before anyone else: "What if we face magic? That will be an issue, with no time mages to support us this time. We have to figure out a way to take out the user, before we lose too many people."

They all started to think, carefully. It was indeed an issue – one which it was imperative to solve; the time mages couldn't always be there to help them, whenever they were in trouble. But, as time passed, and they discussed their ideas, none seemed able to deal with the magic they had seen the enemy using so far.

Liremir suddenly took hold of Malla'ak and looked at him, for permission to speak. Malla'ak made a short statement to the group: "Slave idea. Slave speak."

Liremir stood up and pointed to the map. "What if we distract the magic-caster with arrows, while the miners attack with spikes of rock from underneath. Busy with the arrows, hopefully the caster will not see the attack coming before it's too late. It should work, I think, if we time it correctly and work together."

They all nodded to Liremir. "That could work," agreed Jiri, "if we combine the distraction with an attack from our close combat fighters. We may lose some in that fight, but it should be minimal if we work quickly—"

Malla'ak butted in, not waiting for a gap: "Warriors strong; warriors not die easy. Armour take, armour guard." They all chuckled at that comment, not really knowing its meaning.

Then, they concluded the meeting and started preparing to leave the camp.

Outside, the remaining troops were busy preparing dried meat in water, with dried fruit and vegetables. The mood was still dim, but was growing a little brighter as the food cooked. They chatted and socialized, the bond they had built throughout the journey growing ever stronger. All were sad at every one of the group's losses, and angry at those who had fled and left them behind. For now, though, they focused on the task at hand, knowing that this may well be the last camp they would get to spend together. As the food finished cooking, they eagerly awaited with their bowls, spoons and knives, ready to sit down to eat.

Liremir gladly took a bowl and spoon, tossed in her direction by Malla'ak, then waited for him to serve his own food before taking something for herself, and sitting beside him. It was clear to everyone that there was something more between the two of them than just the usual master/slave relationship.

Turuk seemed to be receiving a rather harsh lesson in manners by Irilie – with great protest, it must be said, yet utterly in vain; Irilie was never the one to back down. Grumbling, Turuk submitted to her mentor, while looking angrily at Irilie, who simply kept a neutral expression as they sat to eat.

Jiri came over with Tirik and Mirak to get food, and they sat down together, to talk and eat. It was apparent that they were beginning to get along quite well.

The socializing seemed to continue into the early evening, before all headed for bed. Many among them suspected that it would be a long day tomorrow, one full of new dangers.

The next day, all got up early, it still being early-dawn and almost dark; the ground was wet with dew. Rations were cooked, the camp packed back up.

Then, on they travelled, ever forward. The Elves quickly went before them, rushing off to scout what lay ahead.

The scouting party of Jiri and the Elves moved quickly, almost like a ballet dance of spring steps. Even were the others moving with their hastiest of steps, they would have been unable to follow.

They moved for what seemed like hours, before they were finally met with what they sought. Close to a hill ahead of them, it was a disturbing sight.

Before them was what could only be described as an army – of what appeared to be corrupt time mages.

The mages were working together, summoning beings out of circles spread out inside a large drawn circle. In the middle of the circles stood Miller, surrounded on all sides by Efors soldiers.

They had fortunately not been spotted, and Jiri signalled his unit to retreat and report their findings – this was not good news, indeed. They quickly made their exit, retreating to report the army before being seen.

The main party of the First Selection Group were making their way to the location when Jiri came running toward them, with his fellow Elves in tow. The party immediately halted, knowing something was wrong before any words were spoken; they waited for the report apprehensively, before moving any farther.

"It is bad news," Jiri confirmed: "an army of Efors soldiers and what appear to be corrupted time mages, ahead of us. They are carrying out some sort of ritual at the sight – we don't know what it is, but it surely can't be good."

Irilie looked at him, poised to speak, but before she was able, Turuk said: "Efors? Those big, red things that my grandfather and mother fought against?"

Irilie looked at her tenderly, nodding confirmation; "I believe so. I only heard tales of them; my predecessor said that they are ten times stronger than Humans."

Malla'ak simply grunted at that. "Me predecessors fought allied them! Me people stronger them; we beat."

Jiri looked at him. "That may be so, but they still very strong. They are mostly brutes, who will smash their way through an army of regular soldiers. But, the corrupt time mages worry me more: they are greater in number, and the one that we saw – Miller – managed to escape last time.

"Still, we may not have magic to support us this time, but I am sure we can handle it. If not, then we need to retreat and regroup."

Mirak and Tirik looked worried. Tirik spoke for them both: "It sounds scary. They can crush us."

"Scary, indeed," agreed Mirak. "Maybe we can make

sinkholes, and just pray they fall in."

Even though they knew it was a joke, they all nodded their agreement at the quip. All knew that the fight ahead would very likely be brutal and costly. But, they must march on, knowing that if they didn't the enemy had already won – and, that they simply couldn't allow; all of their culture, and everything they had built together so far, would collapse if they lost this war, let alone this one fight.

So, they stepped out hastily, their weapons drawn and ready for combat. They were all now in a battle of life or death for their very species.

On the hill, near the ritual site, the First Selection Group arrived, and began to prepare their plan, all the while hoping that the enemy wouldn't attack pre-emptively. But, in this respect, they were to be unlucky.

Miller looked at the aggressors on the hill, before yelling something in a tongue foreign to all of them. While he cast his magic, the Efors soldiers charged the hill, with a full-frontal assault. The First Selection Group quickly scurried into position, and waited for the impact.

The Efors soldiers were fast and tough, breaking through the wall of earthen spikes. Some were impaled on the way, but it did little to stop the charge; most crashed through, clashing with the High Guard and Svambar warriors, who stood firm.

The allies pushed back hard, and the fight was on: a gruelling test of strength and skill versus brute strength. The Elves shot arrows down from above, as rocks and spikes were thrust up from the ground by the miners.

The fight was brutal, with blood spilt all over. The sound of cracking bones mixed in the air, with screams of agony. In short order, the field was a mess of carnage; at least eight Efors soldiers lay dead, alongside two high guards and four Svambar warriors. Blood ran down the hill.

As the battle moved on, it seemed that the First Selection Group was gaining the upper hand, as they slowly pushed back. The Efors soldiers were being picked apart by the arrows, rocks and spikes, and they stumbled all over for respite, some tumbling back down the hill. Soon, they were being forced back and swiftly taken down, as they started to lose their footing.

Seeing the advantage, Turuk cried out to keep pushing. "They are dead! Finish them and deal with the corrupt time mages!"

They rushed forward, with Turuk and Irilie leading the way. Their blood rush grew stronger and stronger.

Miller began to panic, yelling out: "Retreat now! Damn these bastards!" He grabbed four of the mages, pushing them forward; "You four delay them. We will finish our ritual at the base."

As the corrupt time mages made their retreat, the four left behind started to toss their magic at the First Selection Group.

The allies managed to dodge every attack thrown their way, and they split up, the Elves and miners going off in one direction – with Jiri, Tirik and Mirak at their lead – while the last Svambar warriors and High Guard rushed straight on, behind Malla'ak, Liremir, Turuk and Irilie.

The mages focused on the approaching front, hoping to take them down quickly. They didn't get far, though, before arrows from the lightning-fast Elves were raining down on them, distracting just long enough for Liremir to shoot an arrow in the throat of one of them.

The others appeared a touch shaken by this, and it slowed their response. An earthen spike, hurled from distance by one of the miners, suddenly plunged through one the corrupt ones, impaling him. Distracted by this, another got an arrow through his eye.

The last mage, now in a panic, started to frantically channel magic. He didn't get far, before a dagger was hurled into his shoulder by Irilie. Suddenly, Malla'ak was all over the poor time mage, beating him to a pulp.

The fight was over quickly, but the losses were great: only four Svambar warriors remained standing, and three high guards, all badly wounded. The Elves and miners managed to fare better, sustaining only minor injuries. Turuk seemed to be alright, too, but Irilie was in pretty bad shape, having been guarding the child. Malla'ak had a sizeable cut on his head, and Liremir - with a few minor ones of her own - was doing her best to treat her master, with the basic medical equipment they had. Tirik, Mirak and Jiri were all fine, and helping the wounded the best that they could, to prepare them for the journey back home. There was a long road ahead, and there was no telling how many - if any - would make it back.

So, with their wounds treated, they headed a way back, to set up camp and wait out the night, before travelling home. There they would rest, hoping to capture a brief moment in time, before the next fight was ensured, and the war would pick up pace.

But, let us not labour ourselves with another long journey. Let me now return back in time, to events in the Human capital, a month after they had left for their quest.

Before we round off this historical record, I want to tell you the story of the First Selection Army's first regiment...

Chapter Eight

The First Selection Army

The Human capital of Grassiak, a month after the departure of the First Selection Group...

A whole new area was being built in the upper city; Elves, Humans, Svambar and some Demar had joined resources to build the Selection barracks and base.

Scarlet and Amarks, alongside Kraser and a Demar council representative, were standing close by, watching the work progress. "This seems to be going better than I thought," said the Demar. "I guess all races are loyal to the words of their leaders."

Amarks replied calmly: "We can only hope so, Councilman Amuruks."

Kraser looked at them, adding: "Warriors live battle; warriors fight worthy."

A young Elven woman came over to them and bowed before Scarlet, awaiting permission to speak.

"Can we help you?" Scarlet asked her.

The young Elven woman replied: "My name is Erisia. I have been chosen by our captain and our leading Druid to represent our presence, and to ensure the welfare and safety of the Elves who are here." Erisia bowed slightly, to denote her respect.

They greeted her warmly, introducing themselves, before Scarlet returned to business; "Well, it seems that we are almost ready, and can soon begin training, and learning the best ways for us to fight alongside one another."

Kraser nodded; "Training warriors strong; beat more."

They snickered slightly at Kraser's words, though Erisia agreed: "Indeed so. Yet, at least two of these races have never trained a professional army; most here have been militia or guards."

Scarlet nodded her agreement and replied: "That is why the leaders will form the commanding board of this army, and ranks will be discussed once the rest are back from their journey: who will represent each and who will be left in command in their day to day life. As I and Amarks will be busy, I have already sent for the one who will represent the Humans, and will be arriving for training tomorrow."

They all nodded their understanding, agreeing that for now it was probably best to leave things as they were, and deal with issues as they arose in the meantime. The building was progressing, day by day, only ever really slowing when heavy rain or other weather prevented them from their work. The framework was raised within a month, before the outer walls of wood and stone were erected, then a training ground was created. All in, work was scheduled to take three months, with all pitching in, as the current leaders present watched and organized, resolving any disagreements and issues which arose. Within three months, the real training could begin, but it was a long road to get there, and they might not arrive in time.

At the Selection training ground was a young female, in a robe covered with plates. She looked to be around sixteen years old, and was shouting commandingly at the combined army of Demar, Humans, Svambar and Elves.

"I am the Lightors representative, Imilia. I have been chosen to lead training on the First Selection ground, and represent the Humans. Be aware that this is not my first time training soldiers. You have the honour of combining your strengths and weaknesses with those of your allies, in one army. Prove yourselves worthy of being here, and you will deserve to be called Selection soldiers!"

Imilia let the words sink in, before she continued her speech: "When you are at attention, stand straight-backed, with hands at the side. No one speaks, unless spoken to by the highest-ranking presence. You may ask permission to speak, but it will be declined if it bears no relevance to your current exercise or drills. You shall always heed what your commanding officer is saying, and what your orders are, but don't just follow them blindly; use your brain, and understand what they mean, why they are being ordered and the consequences of carrying them out or not. Understand also that all of your actions reflect your own leaders, but first and foremost the Selection.

"This journey will be rough, and it will not be pleasant, but once you have finished training, you will be proud to represent your people and their abilities, and you can feel that you have achieved something most haven't.

"Stand at attention, soldiers, and stand worthy! When I say salute, raise your weapons in a fighting stance. Together!"

All of the First Regiment, counting three-hundred soldiers, stood at attention, adjusting their stance to fight.

Imilia picked up a banner lying nearby, and stuck it firmly into the ground. It depicted an icon of all races resting their hands on top of each other, in black and white; its background was striped with the colours which represented each of the areas they called home: yellow for the Golden Forest; grey for Rroker; green for Grarss; and dark green for Svaplar. Imilia shouted: "Salute the banner of the Selection Army."

All raised their weapons, in a battle-ready pose, pointing in the direction of the banner; Imilia followed suit, doing the same, before shortly yelling: "Attention, soldiers!"

All quickly lowered the weapons, sheathing or holstering them, and stood at attention.

Imilia continued: "We shall practice marching. Keep in mind that some of you are slower, and some are faster than others. Match your march, keep it tight and never let it go. The order shall be so: half of the heavy armour at the front, and the rest with the melee in the back. In the middle, support and range around them. Rearrange, soldiers!"

The soldiers started to scatter, scrambling to get into the right formation, and failing quite badly.

Imilia yelled at them, furiously: "Form order so that you can turn left and march, you bloody idiots!"

The soldiers quickly reformed. After a truly quite awful attempt, Imilia shouted the next command: "Soldiers, left turn. Forward march."

The soldiers followed her directions and started to move. However, the synchronization was terrible, and the formation quickly fell apart.

Imilia started to yell at them, once again: "Come on, soldiers, you can do better than that! You look like fumbling thieves!"

All day long they practiced, failing time and time again. But, gradually, bit by bit, it improved each time they did so – if still far from being of any use. Day turned to evening, before they were permitted to pack up and dismissed, being told to head straight to the barracks to eat, before constructive recreation, then hitting their beds.

The First Regiment went into the barracks and gratefully began to get out of their armour – if they were able; they left it and their weapons on their racks. Then, they went about attending their regular chores: some went to procure cleaning equipment, while others made their way straight to the mess hall, to be first in line for the food; some maintained their equipment.

Despite their good order and general contentment, issues did occasionally arise at times, and the current Selection leaders were always keeping a close eye on them, ready to quickly resolve any problems and, if necessary, deliver punishments where needed. It was tense from the outset, but the mood was slowly starting to turn more favourable, as the different races grew to know and tolerate each other's cultures and personalities.

When the food was served, all scrambled to get their hands on bowls and cutlery with which to eat. But, as time passed, they started to respect each other more, and gradually seemed to forget the petty scuffles and fights for food. When they sat down to eat, peace came over them at last and, just for a little while, they could relax.

When done eating, most hit the racks, knowing very well that a tough new day awaited, and a lot of drilling, starting early in the morning. Another day of practice; of learning how to work as a team, and not just within one's own racial and cultural military forces. They were in a combined army now, where all must learn to fit in, to learn the rules and regulations, and to accept one another.

The current leaders all stayed in the barracks, or near to it, to be ready to deal with any cultural issues at a moment's notice, and to ensure that all learned not to entertain them. The gates to the barracks were closed at night, to ensure no one deserted without their knowledge.

The next morning, at the Selection barracks...

It was already well past breakfast, when the noise of things being toppled, yelling and shouting could be heard all over the barracks. Imilia, along with Erisia, Kraser and Amuruks, came running down from upstairs, to see what the racket was all about.

On one side of the dining hall stood a small group of Svambar warriors; on the other side some young Elves, nearby whom were a number of young Human males. The Elves, Humans and Svambar were squaring up, shouting back and forth at each other. A collective of Demar miners sat nearby, quietly watching them with amusement. Racist slurs, accusations and insults were being thrown all over the place, while bowls, spoons and even chairs were being tossed back and forth.

Kraser immediately rushed over to the Svambar warriors and, before they knew it, he bundled two of them onto the ground, before staring down their cronies. Erisia made the sound of a bird's whistle, and the Elves went still on the spot, while Imilia was content with simply walking by the Humans, to afford them a strong glare of disappointment, which made them tense up. Amuruks, knowing full well the apathy of his own people, just went over to the corner to join them.

Imilia was the first to speak out: "What in Times' name is going on here? And, why are you destroying Selection property, you insolent worms?!"

Each of the three groups involved began pouring out their excuses, raising their voices to counter and defend; before long, the racial slurs and the arguments had again picked up.

Kraser was starting to lose his temper, it seemed, and he suddenly yelled out to the Svambar warriors: "You not worthy warrior! You dishonour kingska! Honour join. Punishment dealt!" The Svambar warriors seemed a little annoyed by the dressing down, and began to grumble insolently.

Erisia was equally angry, though she managed to keep a calm tone, resembling more a teacher in a classroom full of kids. "You call yourself Elves? You behave like Corrupted Elves . You dare to insult the sacrifices your previous hyr made to ensure your survival, and that you can live and thrive together, without being enslaved. Your behaviour is a disgrace to your people." The Elves' faces dropped and hung heavy, covered by the signs of shame and guilt.

Imilia had calmed down enough to resume type character, and imparted her drill instructor's tone to the Humans: "You dare to disobey the orders and agreements that your king and queen have worked so hard to achieve over so many years? You dare to besmirch all that they have built, through bloodshed and the tears of torn apart families and lost friends?" The Humans shook in fear and embarrassment, as they could only but look at Imilia.

Amuruks spoke up from the corner of the room, and his words were a shock to his fellow Demars: "It seems that my people did nothing to stop them, so by complicity they are responsible also. I suggest twenty lashes to those directly involved, and ten to each of those who observe without intervention."

The leaders reluctantly nodded their agreement, and the trainees were marched outside for a lesson, being told to call together the whole First Selection Army First Regiment on the way.

The people involved in the fight were each bound between two poles, by their fellow soldiers, to await their fate. Imilia stood back with a whip in her hand, as the other soldiers were gathered to watch the punishment. Erisia, Amuruks and Kraser each carried a whip also, as they waited their turn, for no leader was permitted under the treaty to physically discipline a soldier of another race.

Imilia bellowed across the formation, with a stern and serious tone: "Soldiers of the Selection Army, watch and learn as we drill this lesson into your heads, by the blood and tears and screams of your comrades in arms. They dared to insult each other – to insult their allies – not to mention disgracing their own race. Well, soldiers, all will learn a lesson you won't easily forget: we will not tolerate this behaviour.

"When we are done dispensing the punishment, the trainees will walk – or, drag themselves – around the perimeter of the city and back here, so that all may receive the message. Let the lesson begin."

Imilia turned around and nodded to her fellow leaders, as they started to hammer down their whips at the recipient nearest to them, focusing attention for the count of twenty (or ten, of course, in the case of Amuruks), before moving on to the next. The sound of the cracking whips, and the agonized squealing of the poor soldiers, filled the grounds of the Selection barracks.

The soldiers, filed in formation as they watched on, were undoubtedly frightened by the sight; some even held back tears, while others just stood and watched apathetically, enduring the emotional train wreck.

Within a matter of minutes, which felt much longer, it was over. The whipped soldiers were released from their bonds and pushed or dragged by their comrades, forced onward, as they walked the outskirts of the city. Those who had taken twenty lashes left dripping trails of blood on the path, while the punished Demar soldiers limped painfully after them. Still, their representatives forced them onward.

After returning to the barracks, what seemed like hours later, the injured men were given only five minutes to clean up and change, before they were being tutored in hand to hand combat by Kraser. Bruising and lacerations occurred easily, as they learned that a fresh injury is very vulnerable to worsening. Still, though, they were forced onward, earning no more than a five-minute break, after two hours of fighting.

Following that, they were charged with keeping their gear in fighting order, by Amuruks, before a final two-hour lesson in tactical planning by Erisia.

Eventually, finally, they were allowed to call it a day, being dismissed to the barracks for dinner and rest. Some of them passed out before dinner was served.

But, it wasn't an easy day for the rest of the recruits, either. Training was tough, with discipline high, and throughout the day, only rations and water had been issued. Compounded by the harsh lesson they had been taught early in the day, by that evening three Elves, three Svambar warriors, four Humans and two Demar had dropped out, finding the training just too hard – and, they had no desire for this kind of lifestyle. After their resignations, they weren't allowed to say goodbye to their friends, but instead quickly escorted out, with what little pay they had earnt, left to make their own way home, as the gates were closed unceremoniously behind them.

But, for the others, as the months dragged on, even as the training became harder and tougher, it somehow became easier to endure and to learn. They were toughening up. They were learning how to use their strengths, as compensation for their weaknesses. Only a further four of each race dropped out in total, and that was something to be proud of.

They were the First Regiment of the First Selection Army, and that was absolutely an honour. They were the best on offer, not just of their race, but of all the races.

Finally, after long, hard training, it was their last duty to attend as trainees: their passing out ceremony, at which they received the now coveted badge and surcoat featuring the same image and colour scheme as the banner.

It was a glorious moment for them all, and they were permitted a temporary lapse in discipline to celebrate and congratulate each other.

But, no sooner was the ceremony complete that a Human messenger came riding into the Selection barracks, with blood dripping from gaping arrow wound.

"First Regiment, the border to the lands of the Humans is under heavy assault," he blurted quickly, lest he pass out from exhaustion first; "the local garrison cannot hold out. We need reinforcements!"

And, with that, the rider fell from his horse and relaxed, gasping out a breath which would in fact turn out to be his last.

Erisia checked him over and sighed, sadly. "Dark Elven poison."

The command to prepare for battle was given. Horses and carts were packed with tents, rations and all the gear needed, and within the hour, the army had started to depart, as one, out of the gates. Formation was as practiced, and they moved in a swift march.

Heading out of the city, they were joined by a small unit of high guards, with Scarlet and Amarks at the lead, greeting them as they marched to war. Drums played alongside them, providing the rhythm and tempo of their progress. A messenger was quickly sent south, to find and inform the First Selection Group of the events.

A day later, the First Selection Group was travelling home through Rroker, almost at the border of Grarss, when the messenger arrived to give them word of the attack on the Humans.

They quickly agreed to march toward it, with all haste, hoping that they might turn the tide of war. They had no idea if they would make any difference, or even if they would make it in time. They hoped the First Regiment could hold out until they arrived.

A month later.

A border post stood in the middle ground, between Barlar and Grarss, surrounded by pointed logs dug into a wall of earth and rocks, and a moat cut into the ground around it. Now, it was almost completely overrun by Efors soldiers, Corrupted Elves and some rebel forces of Svambar and Humankind. They were still there when the First Regiment arrived to engage them.

Led by Scarlet and Amarks, along with their High Guard, the Selection army quickly set off at attack speed, leaving the carts behind them. Surprised, the enemy saw the charge and the Svambar and Human factions immediately retreated, as did the Corrupted Elves . The Efors soldiers stood firm and waited.

The First Regiment carved a bloody path through the enemy's shield of Human soldiers, now trying in vain to fire off their spring-loaded bows, or counterattack with melee weapons. The Elves of the First Regiment reached them first, glaives moving in front of the many Elven archers, who sent volley upon volley toward the enemy. Many fell instantly, as the First Regiment soldiers caught up and clashed with them.

The enemy was quickly overrun. Although they managed to wound some of the First Regiment frontline, the battle was undoubtedly won. There was a bloody price for the enemy: a company of sixty Human pawns lay dead, as did many Efors,

Corrupted Elves and other various rebel forces.

Scarlet stood in the middle of the bloodbath and yelled her orders: "Get the towers patched up, repair the wall and prepare for a siege. Those bastards aren't entering these lands without paying the price in blood. Stand firm, take care of the wounded and ensure our victory!" The beaten and bruised forces cheered, as they immediately got to work.

The corner towers had survived the Efors attack – barely – and were quickly patched up; the holes in the walls were filled with anything which lay in sight – gruesomely, this happened to be the corpses of the enemy.

Within an hour, the enemy had returned in force, mostly consisting of Efors and Corrupted Elves , though there were small numbers of Humans and Svambar among them. They camped just outside the range of the archers, much to the annoyance of Scarlet. She dismounted and made her way to the top of the wall.

"Come on, you cowards! Fight us – I dare you, you ignorant little otherworld force!"

Amarks walked over to her, putting a hand on her shoulder. "Easy, dear. They'll come, and when they do we'll beat them to a pulp."

Scarlet mumbled something incoherent, then started yelling out her orders: "Imilia, Erisia, Amuruks and Kraser, set up the camp and prepare for battle at any moment. Do not let this place fall!"

The calls came back in turn:

Kraser: "Me got it."

Amuruks: "Right, right; on it."

Imilia: "As you command, Queen Scarlet."

Erisia: "Understood."

The forces quickly set to work, as the respective orders were relayed to them. Tents were set up and sleeping skins put in place, while Scarlet and Amarks kept watch, until the forces started a guarding routine on the walls, waiting for the enemy to attack.

But, day turned to night, and nothing happened.

Becoming more and more annoyed and restless from the wait, Scarlet shouted across the camp: "Leaders, gather in my tent for planning."

The leaders quickly assembled in Scarlet and Amarks's big white tent, which had been hastily set up in the middle of the camp. Kraser, Amuruks, Erisia and Imilia stepped inside and saluted, before walking to the table set in the middle, Scarlet and Amarks standing over it.

As they gathered around, Scarlet tapped the tabletop and spoke: "Right, the enemy is boldly camped outside of our walls, likely waiting for reinforcements, or for our wounded to die. So, fresh in the morning, we need to have our ballistas up and running, and start to bombard their camp; I would rather strike now, than wait for them to finish whatever it is they are preparing. How can we do this without drawing too much attention, or losing any of the ballistas, since the walls are beaten up, and the moats are filled?" She looked at Erisia.

Thoughtfully, Erisia took two wooden blocks, representing archers, from her belt bag, placing them just beneath the walls. "If we place the Elven archers just underneath the walls, the enemy won't know where they are, or where they are shooting from. On the walls, place the Human spring-loaded shooters as far back as you can, since they have better armour which can withstand long-distance shots. Arm them strategically with the four ballistas we brought with us."

Imilia brought out two warrior blocks, placing one in front of one of the archers on the wall, and one near the gate. "Place the

Svambar warriors in front of the range, for cover, while the High Guard are placed near the gate; should any try to enter, we must be able to reinforce quickly."

Kraser nodded, without adding anything. Amuruks, however, pulled out two blocks, one portraying a Demar miner, the other a robed figure; he placed them close to the Elves.

"If we hide the priests and Demar miners near the Elves, they can provide hidden support, and give the enemy a nasty surprise." Scarlet and Amarks nodded, approvingly.

"Very well," said Amarks. "It seems that we have a plan of sorts. If we are all in agreement, then I say we get the ballistas assembled, and the army ready for early morning."

They all nodded their agreement, and started to leave.

Early the next morning, the First Regiment was organized according to the battleplan of last night. It was still somewhat dark, but the light was improving by the minute.

On the walls of the border post, Humans stood ready with the ballistas, waiting for orders, along with the Svambar warriors; the bladirs guarded the front, anxious to get the battle underway.

Scarlet raised her hand, waiting for what seemed an eternal moment, before finally lowering it. The ballistas ignited the first bolts and fired them, right into the heart of the enemy camp. The impact set the camp ablaze, and the enemy scrambling, but this quickly turned into counter-attack.

The enemy moved swiftly, bombarding the gate with a hail of arrows, bolts and rocks from their base. As the red brutes quickly started to break down the already damaged gate, sending huge, wooden splinters flying into the air, the High Guard, along with other Human forces of the First Regiment, quickly formed a wedge, with Scarlet and Amarks in the middle.

The Efors quickly crashed through the gate, ramming their way through the wedge formation, splitting it wide open. But, they were easy pickings for the Demar people's rock spikes, and the Elves' arrows. The fight was a brutal melee, with soldiers sent flying from the force of the Efors attack.

Yet, the enemy paid the price, as more and more of them fell, one by one, from the arrows and spikes of rock. They weren't as good in formation, nor as organized as the Selection soldiers and the High Guard, and it was on display clearly, as the enemy fell. Still, there were losses and casualties on both sides.

Then, just as the battle seemed to be going the way of the defenders, the worst happened: one of the enemies knocked Amarks down, striking a club-like weapon across his head so hard that the skull could be heard cracking open.

With a squeal, Scarlet tried desperately to defend him, before two arrows suddenly embedded into her armpit; as she staggered, she received the same club around the head as her husband; the same sound of her skull splitting accompanied the blow.

At the sight of the queen's fall, the defenders' morale started to plummet like a house of cards – only the Svambar troops and the Elves stood their ground. But, spirits had fallen so low now, and were so badly damaged, that it was apparent they would not be repaired, and the battle was surely lost. The Selection army began to disperse.

Yet, Imilia refused to surrender to the chaos. Going up the tower – killing her way there – she began to sing. Her voice sounded like a pair of monks, in a troubadour tone, yet with one combined voice:

"Stand up, soldiers;
stand and rise to the deed.
Let not fear nor panic set your heart.

Faith is with us – be our guide.
We shall not fear the dark –
fear whatever we can't see.
Today we stand, on the brink of losing;
leaders fall and yet soldiers rise.
Steel your heart,
steel your mind;
let them not pass to our families;
let them not conquer us.
Rise to the deed, brave soldiers of all,
and we shall see the dawn again;
see our family and friends,
meeting them as heroes –
heroes that saved their daily life,
that saved their existence.
Rise to the deed, men and women all."

And, as the song echoed out of the tower, the fleeing soldiers stopped in their tracks and turned. Slowly, they started to return to the battle.

Morale was rising tangibly, as the song continued. And, the longer they heard it, the harder they started to fight, with thoughts of their families and friends now at the forefront of their minds. They fought, even though, as the battle raged back and forth, it seemed an ever-present fact that they would lose.

Suddenly, there was movement over the horizon, and a cheer went up: the First Selection Group had arrived, and was advancing at full speed.

Malla'ak, Liremir, Irilia and Turuk rode out in front, with the remaining Svambar warriors and High Guard. Jiri, Mirak and Tirik were right behind them, along with the Elves and the rest of the Demar miners. It was barely a moment before they were rushing into battle.

When Turuk saw her mother and father lying on the ground,

both of their heads smashed inside their dented helmets, she screamed. Furious, she rushed the enemy with a roar, leaving Irilia and the High Guard desperately exerting themselves to keep up with her. Malla'ak and the Svambar warriors had already engaged the forward enemy, Liremir sticking close to her master, to cover him with arrows.

Jiri gathered the Elves to fire a volley of arrows or defend the range, while Mirak and Tirik stayed nearby, sending rock spikes from the ground, and earth attacks at the enemy.

The whole battlefield was engulfed by chaos. Soldiers fell all over, left and right – both those of the combined races and of the enemy. But, once again, the enemy was quickly overwhelmed by their lack of organization – and by the willpower of their enemies. They were quickly pushed back and forced into a hasty retreat.

As they did so, none followed them outside the border post, so tired and wounded were they all. Instead, they roared out a victory cry.

The death toll on the side of the combined army was close to six-hundred, with four-hundred wounded. The enemy, however, lost nearly two-thousand, with many more lying wounded. It was a strategic and costly victory for the allies, particularly so for a queen and king having fallen, but it was a victory, and that was all that mattered.

I shall tell you of what happened after the battle…

The Humans returned to the capital, with the bodies of their queen and king. The rest of the fallen were buried at a newly dug mass gravesite, among the many others buried near the border post.

A whole two months of grieving followed the elaborate burial ceremony of the queen and king. Irilia was put in charge of affairs, until Turuk exceeded the rank of squire. She is now the queen-in-waiting, being groomed for her rule; still, it is Irilia whom she consults, and who guides many of the decisions.

Imilia left the Selection to form a new order, and a new lead officer was chosen for the Humans at the barracks.

The Elves summoned their Druids and planted trees over the bodies of the fallen Elves, making the gravesite a beauty to behold, as well as a grim reminder of what happened – and what may yet come.

After returning home, to grieve their dead and secure the forest, the Svambar people made a feast to celebrate the fallen warriors, and to acknowledge that they lived and died as heroes.

The Demar people who returned home to the mines spoke of their deeds, and would often compare their adventures to the life of mining. Tirik and Mirak, however, joined the Selection, always unable to resist curiosity and seek new adventures. Later, they would join Imilia as priestesses of Demar – but that is a story for another time.

The races carry on their lives. The ongoing war necessitates a lot of meetings, and the town criers are perpetually busy, spreading the news.

Now, I will provide further insight into the races themselves...

The Races

ELVES

The Elves are tall creatures, all in the range of 2-2.5 metres; they are very slim, though densely muscled. Their hair is of a silvery-grey or a golden-blonde, and their ears resemble those of the Humans, though topped with a tip, rather than rounded. And, like the tips of those silly, long ears, Elves' eyes also differ from Humans': they are yellow, and able to see in darkness.

Elves age slowly, and can live as long as three-thousand years! In fact, they are still viewed as children anywhere up to the age of two-hundred; teens are considered between the ages of two-hundred and four-hundred; an Elf is not considered an adult until reaching over four-hundred years old. The elders, despite being over two-thousand years old, are not easy to discern from other adults; they never grow older in looks than when they reach their peak, at four-hundred years.

Elves worship the forest gods, whom they know by the names Methora, Fatharna and Lidyar. Unknown to the Elves, the first two of those gods are actually long dead, and succeeded by those they would call their son and daughter, whom I brought to be alongside me, along with Lidyar.

They use weapons of stone, earth or wood, but they never cut it or pick it from source; rather, they use what they find on the ground, or what is offered to them, according to their beliefs, by the forest gods. They hunt, but do so with great respect for the animal's spirit. The hides of their prey are used for armour, protected with beeswax and threaded with leaves.

Their gods are worshipped by Druids, who rarely speak anything other than the native tongue, and a form of ancient Elven, which even I don't know the meaning of. Except for their leader, Druids possess the one big social drawback of being completely naked, and will hug every tree, stone formation or hill they see in their bare skin; this is the way they believe that they worship their gods. The leader of the Druids is known as Druor.

Elves possess unknown magic, which allows them to disappear into a mist, or to move faster than others. They can also do many other things, but most of these are unknown to me at this moment, I must confess.

They don't care about gender; some are even known to be both male and female. All carry arms to defend the forest, and may take any work that they wish. They have no standing army, but all Elves are part of the Dieferdar, a sort of militia, which is very highly trained; training takes place daily, for around two hours.

The Elves lay down their dead underneath trees, believing that they will become one with it, and will guide their people, or protect natural places. Kings are laid to rest underneath a king's tree. None knows for sure what that is, though I am aware that its culture believes that a king's tree provides the wisdom to rule. They live and make their home in the middle of the Golden Forest.

Elven langue is broad, and full of strange words and phrases. I will do my best to try writing it for you.

The langue of the Elves:

Da-ra-ri : of.

Kin-nar : peace, or *of* peace, if in a title.

Ir : who.

To-rein : are.

Tiri : great.

Ji-ri : high.

Hyr Tiri Darari Kinnar : Great King of Peace.

Men-ty-a : you.

Mo-gein : me.

Fe-lan : friend.

I-ty : find.

Ea-ra-si-ra : "where the people prosper."

Die-fer-dar : defenders of the woods.

Hyr-ty-ar : king of the forest.

Trre-on : forest.

Scar-vir : guides.

Tris : this.

Evir : evil.

Ta-ro-ga : Elven.

Fre-yar : fear.

Hyr : king.

Hu-mir : Human.

Tar : forest.

Hyr Humir : King of Humans.

Ty-ar : forest.

Me-tho-ra : "mother of earth and stone."

Fa-thar-na : "father of forest and earth."

Li-dy-ar : "lady of water and air."

A-ro-mi-ror : armour.

Mea-ti : mighty.

Fa-ri : father.

Vin-ga-ra : prince.

En-va : son.

Co-ma-ra : journey.

Ty-o : yes.

Gre-fyih : greetings.

Ly-ior : late.

Sy-oair : sorry.

Wi-yen-po : we.

Dre-nod : Druid.

Dy-oy : did.

Io-tiy : a lot.

Foiy : of.

Ryia : captain.

Cli-joa : cure.

Loa-doin : land.

Fra-om : from.

Fores-tho-pu-tye : gods of the forest.

E-for-gor : Elf-slave punisher.

Wyen : were.

Boj-hu : born.

Druor : Great Father/Mother/Druid.

Erand : and.

Skio-pua : spirit.

Ment-yag : your.

Woy : will.

Tearch : teacher or mentor.

Bom-lo : be.

Ror-bur : reborn.

I-tryn : again.

Bre-kon : borrow.

Ef-lar : Elves.

Sta-civ : stand.

U-mi-ra : united.

A-pre : and.

Shi-ume : show.

Ru-hir : ready.

To-grer : together.

Arti : against.

To-pri : with.

Fram : for.

Ny-me-re : number.

Trre : tree.

Ariski : "Sword of the Forest."

Fra-om Trre-on men-ty-a wy-en Boj-hu e-rand fra-om trre-on men-ty-ag ski-o-pu-a woy bom-lo ror-bur : "From the tree you were born and thus your spirit will be reborn a tree again."

Gre-fyihs Tar. Por-ple. A-mer, alle-ice gran va-lan-taar, fu-or u-nert A-rom-iror Por-ple. Gar-at Grassiak. If-ror, par-te-ren : "Greetings, great people. I have great news: any volunteer who wishes can join a combined army with the people of our allies. Gather at Grassiak if you wish to be part of it."

Here, I will end my profile of the Elves, and move on to a perhaps simpler one: the Human.

HUMANS

The Humans in the Land Between Times bear little difference to any other Humans, except that they grow no taller than 170cm. Often densely muscled, due to training, yet they can also be fat, wide, or indeed any peculiar sort of body shape. Their hair colour can vary, though men always keep it short, above the ear, and women mid-length to long, though in any variant style of that rule.

Their faith is in Lightors, the god of Light. His priests and priestesses, of the Order of Torsfor, use Lightors's gift as a power, to spread joy and heal the injured. The order has its own holy military force, though it is primarily charged with funeral ceremonies, by burial in earth or burning.

Humans make their home in the fertile land of Grarss.

DEMAR PEOPLE

Next, we shall take a look at the Demar people.

Short and prudish, this mining people are a sub-race of the Humans. Growing from just one metre to four feet in height, they are usually broad and muscular. But, one key thing which differentiates them from Human is the lack of hair; they never have beards, and are usually bald or very short-haired.

They believe that their mountain home of Demar gave them the power to shape rocks and earth to their will. Thus was born their name and their culture, both stipulating that they put their dead inside the mountain, in sealed tombs, in the belief that the mountain would take them. As you have already read, their home of the Demar Mountain is in the rocky land of Rroker.

SVAMBAR PEOPLE

Let us now move on to the Svambar people – as much only as I know about them.

Svambar people are a creature crossbred from a mixture of Orc and Human – yet there will soon likely be more species in their lineage, if continues their practice of taking and bedding slaves of other races. They can vary the biological traits of their respective ancestors; for example, there may be one of their race with a wide, Orc-like upper body and the slimmer build of a Human, and another which may be the other way around.

They walk or run in a crouched stance, with knees bent, and

can only straighten up when standing; it is impossible for them to run or walk in an upright position. When standing up straight, at full height, they can vary from seven to eight feet tall.

The Svambar keep slaves as a sign of status and power, although their slaves must only be volunteers, or sentenced to subservience for committing an offence. They worship a creature of the swamps, whom they call Measeri, and they are born warriors; they believe that to die in battle is the highest honour, whilst to die in indolence is a disgrace. The warriors are put into the ground or burned, whilst the rest are tossed into the swamp-covered land of Svaplar, where they make their home.

Here are some of the words and phrases I observed of their curious tongue:

Emeary thuse maste gauer : "May the swamps open a path of guidance."

Took Ma, an-vach : "Forward; march to battle!"

ke Svam-bar Ir-ke, War-ca. War-ra-ga, Ma vach : "We Svambar great warriors. March battle."

Here follows a final description of the current enemy forces…

THE EFORS

The Efors' forces are rather unknown to me, though from what I been told by my mage, who spoke with the hyr of the Elves, they are masters from the darkest dimension, where only the strong rule, and the weak are enslaved.

They are well over three metres tall; their skin we have seen, so far, is a tone of red. The Efors are more brute than intelligence. Yet, this brute force has enabled them to conquer several dimensions; even despite the fact that they always struggle when faced with an enemy which thinks. They are known to subject other races to doing their fighting for them, yet treat their subservients like livestock; only a very selected few manage to earn their respect.

There is not much else I know about these people, as those who have survived them are few, and even fewer still wish to talk about their experience. I dare say I shall find out more in the future – and in doing so, may hope to save my lovely land.

*

Here, I will end this volume of tales, with a small glimpse into what came next. May time preserve you all, until the next time...

In an unknown forest location, a small, blackish-purple Elf was peeking through the bushes, with piercing purple eyes, when he heard a call:

"Birisi, come home before our masters find us in the forbidden area."

The tiny Elf darted off, disappearing into the forest.

...